THE CALL OF DUST

BOOK ONE OF THE ARAT SERIES

M. R. SAINT

DRAMATIS PERSONAE

The Arat - orphan girl seer mage

Khiron - sworn protector of the Arat

The Raja - Ruler of Ceidon

Philomene the Guileless - Advisor to The Raja

Master of Swords - the Sword of Ceidon

The Nnsesutee - blind swordsman

Zatrin Bei - a Sibulla

Yaisen'Re Bennu - a royal of the Suten kingdom

Neftii - a Suten mage

The Sibulla - arbiter of the kingdoms of Gaia

The Ulaan - an undefated warrior culture

The Suten - a numinous island kingdom

THE CALL OF DUST

BOOK ONE OF THE ARAT SERIES

Names: Saint, M. R., author.

Title: The Call of Dust/M. R. Saint

Identifiers: ISBN 978-1-7340142-0-4 (paperback) | ISBN 978-1-7340142-2-8 (ebook)

Subjects: | BISAC: FICTION / Fantasy / Epic. | EPIC. | FICTION / Action & Adventure. | FICTION / Science Fiction / Adventure. | GSAFD: Fantasy fiction.

Paperback ISBN 978-1-7340142-0-4

Published in the US by Liquid Black Press, an imprint of Liquid Black LLC.

Editor: Chersti Nieveen

Cover: Roger Creus Dorico roger.creus@digitalrowye.com

For Mark-Daniel and Noni

$$1$$

ARAT

The Kingdom of Zaim

Near the end of the Third Age

Crouched beneath the low outcropping of a sunken shanty, Khiron clutched his dagger's hilt as he watched four men in hooded, green-flecked cloaks, hastily move through the dusky trails of the Dun Quarter toward his position. Their hoods were in constant motion, three of the four keeping watch as they penetrated the heart of the old campground where the poorest of the kingdom found refuge.

The Dun Quarter was a sprawling area of dirt and jutting rocks; an area where nothing grew but the most stubborn of weeds and thorny bushes, populated with low-roofed shanties which housed the poorest of the farmers. He imagined that from the heights of Mount Ceidon, from which they came, it must have looked like an island of barrenness surrounded by hundreds of acres of manicured verdant green. It was easily an hour march at a quick-step from the Mount, so he knew they must be fatigued, although they showed no signs of it.

The men walked briskly across the barren dust, their footing sure as they navigated the disjointed landscape. A wide trench became visible as they approached it, the buzzing of flies filling the air. Noses flared as they were assaulted by the stench of urine-soaked excrement. The rotting corpse of a deer lay atop the manure in the scorching suns. Hands quickly reached into hoods as they hurried on, covering their mouths and noses as they followed the route of the trench towards their goal.

Despite his irritation, he found himself grinning. The Arat had said that men from Mount Ceidon would come and had instructed him to wait here for them. He had held reservations about the wisdom of the command but kept them silent. She was the reason that he had come to this land, although he hadn't known that when he came. He had since sworn his sword and life into her service. Her sight of future timelines was as sharp as any that he had ever heard of who had the gift, and as of yet, he had not regretted his decision. He had asked her how he would recognize them, and she had just smiled and turned away. Now he knew why.

The men stood out like shiny blades reflecting sunlight. Their movements were uniform, as those trained to operate in a regiment. Their cloaks were functional but showed no signs of wear or the discoloration that came from extended exposure to the elements, and he doubted that boots of that quality could be purchased anywhere in the lowlands. If they were attempting stealth, they were incompetent at best. Either that or they felt that lowlanders were too stupid to notice. He spat. How like the high-born to consider themselves better and smarter than the masses. The sooner he intercepted them, the better.

He emerged from his hiding spot and they stopped as one, jeweled hilts suddenly visible. He raised his hands with his palms empty. "Fear not! I am sent from the Arat to guide you to her, O welcomed guests from Mount Ceidon. That is why you have come, yes?" He looked at each of them eye to eye in turn to show his sincerity. His expression remained hopeful as he glanced at his hands. "May I?"

The lead soldier, eyes dark as coals and cropped brown hair which lay flat against his sweaty forehead, nodded with a menacing stare. "Slowly, and where we can see them."

"I'm carrying a dagger but nothing else," Khiron said, lowering his arms. "I pose no threat to you."

"He knows who we are," a voice came from the man that the others seemed to be protecting, his face chubby with large eyes. "The Arat demonstrates her abilities to us to give confidence that we have done the right thing in coming. It is well." He motioned and the men's hilts disappeared behind their cloaks. "What is your name?"

"My name is Khiron," he said slowly, the tension in his shoulders abating. "I am a sword sworn in the Arat's service."

"We bear respect to your office," the chubby-faced man said with a smile, "and to the respect you grant us in not bringing your sword. The honor is not overlooked, nor minimized." He nodded to Khiron in a genuine acknowledgement. "Please, lead the way."

He gave a deep bow to the speaker and led them away from the trench and into a cluster of one-story shanties that lay to the West.

We are on their way with no blood spilled, he thought. *As always, she was right.*

A breeze from the Silver Sea reached them, the twin suns becoming partially obscured by lazy clouds stretched like pulled cotton in the wind. The scent of salt washed over the land like crisp, cool water.

Sounds of life began to surround them as people became visible. Barefoot children playing without restraint: many chasing one another while others skipped rope or fought in mock sword duels with sticks.

Men and women hung clothes on thin ropes that were attached from roof to roof. Iron nails that bent upwards at their base bit deep into wood and mortar, anchoring the network of ropes which seemed to pull the mix-match of shanties — some square, some round — into a unified community.

Hides were beaten, armor hammered in open-air shops, clothes were sown, and gamblers gathered in clusters: men and women alike calling out numbers and shapes; some with zeal, others in despair. Together, the sound created a tapestry that muted the squalor that surrounded them and created a sense of vitality; of community.

Khiron guided them through the paths and thoroughfares with seasoned familiarity. Angling northwest by the suns arc, they reached an area filled with dirt-faced children. He stopped, then moved to the side with arms outstretched towards the children.

The four men stopped, a look of suspicion on the lead soldier's face, confusion writ on the others.

The children looked up and ran away with giggles and laughter, leaving a short and chubby girl that looked to be no older than ten or eleven, squatting and picking up stones. An empty space beside her right front tooth glared at them as she smiled.

"Those who seek you have arrived," Khiron said. He took a position behind her and stood wide-legged, with his hands clasped behind him.

"This is the Arat?" the lead soldier sneered. "He has played us for newborns!"

"Silence, Jittan," the chubby-faced man said. "This is indeed the Arat. I can sense her power."

The girl turned to the speaker, looked at his round face and clear eyes, and smiled. "You are a mage." Her voice was young and had yet to find itself, her eyes youthful and full of wonder. "None other than the Great Raja's advisor, Philomene, I see. I am honored that you have come."

The soldiers tensed, reaching for their swords, but stood down at the wave of Philomene's hand.

"I must confess," he said in a hush, "you are not what I expected."

The Arat giggled with the unfeigned freedom of youth. "Those with titles seldom are. Wouldn't you agree, Philomene the Guileless?"

His eyes tightened momentarily and then he relaxed as he chuckled. "Unrobed truth is even more rare, young seer. Is it youth that leaves your thoughts unrestrained, or the power of your calling?"

"Time will tell, great mage. Unfortunately, time is not something that we have to spare." She came to her feet and dusted off the knees of her trousers. When she lifted her eyes up to Philomene again, all mirth was gone. "Our kingdom is under threat."

His eyes widened, and they held no unbelief. He moved passed his guards to sand before her and lowered his hood. "What have you seen, young seer? Leave nothing out." His guards took positions behind him: two facing outward, Jittan taking a post beside him, watching the Arat and Khiron with undisguised disgust.

Khiron watched the guard's eyes, and shifted closer to the Arat, positioning the sheathe of his dagger on an angle that would give him the easiest access to pull and throw in a single motion.

If the Arat noticed Jittan's disposition, she didn't show any sign.

"I have seen an army approaching. A people of dual-hued skin: one side half pale blue, the other tanned gold—"

"Dris' beard," Philomene said. "The Ulaan." The blood drained from his face as he interrupted her. With haste, he looked around to see if he had been overheard.

She paused in what seemed to be puzzlement and reached out to comfort him when Jittan unsheathed his sword and advanced. "No commoner may touch my Lord!"

Khiron's hand slipped to his dagger hilt. He tensed to throw it, and then froze in utter shock.

Completely unflustered, the Arat had moved towards the attacking soldier and appeared to lightly slap Jittan's mailed stomach with her opened palm. The guard flew back three full body-lengths as if struck with a battering ram.

It took everyone by surprise. The other two guards, whose backs were turned, drew their swords looking for an enemy, turning left to right in quick succession. Seeing no one other than the Arat, Khiron, and their master, they paused in confusion. Philomene's voice brought everyone into focus.

"Stand down immediately," he said angrily to his guards. "Check on Jittan and see if there is anything you can do for him." He turned to the seer. "I beg your forgiveness, Arat. My lead guardsman has overstepped his bounds and has offended my honor."

She sighed, for the first time looking older than her eleven years. "I take no offense. Many of you who live on the Mount hold our status in disregard. This was regrettable, but the possibility was foreseen." That her words were incongruous with her age gave them a sense of weight which brokered no argument.

The lines on Khiron's face grew sharp as he stood behind her, though he tried hard to conceal his feelings. The Arat had known that she would be attacked and hadn't told him. Despite the result, he would have to speak to her about this, and soon. And how had she done that? He had never seen her doing anything like it before. The thought gripped around his intestines and squeezed.

Philomene the Guileless stood still, his eyes becoming unfocused, his head tilted towards Jittan's motionless body.

"He yet lives, Honorable Philomene," the Arat said hurriedly. "He will have a nasty bruise on his back where the earth struck him, but he is merely unconscious." There was mirth in her voice, but it didn't reach her eyes.

"I am in your debt, gifted one," he said as his questing confirmed her words. His eyes refocused. "Again, I ask your forgiveness. Speak what we can do to make amends, and if it is within my power, it will be so."

Head shaking in irritation, she spoke, a hint of pleading in her voice. "We don't have time for this. I did not wait for you to come to be delayed by decorum." She glanced at Khiron, then she turned back to the mage.

Philomene flinched at the expression on her face. "Forgive me. I believe that I understand. Please tell me, what else did you see?"

She looked at him for a long moment before her expression became resolute. Putting her palms together, she opened them a crack and looked within as if hiding a coin or a bauble from a curious friend.

When she looked up, her eyes were filled with tears. "Too much...I see too much."

She turned from the mage and pointed to a log that lay about five steps from them. "Khiron, your sword lies within. Collect it and all your things. We sleep near the docks and take the first ship from port as the suns rise. Meet me at the known place in one bell."

Khiron bowed and moved quickly, collecting his sword and glancing back towards the unmoving Jittan before disappearing into the shadows of the shanties. Finding a good space to hear with a line of sight, he stopped and kept watch. Despite who she was, he'd be damned if he would leave her completely unprotected. Whatever she had done to the soldier, he had a lurking suspicion that she wouldn't be able to do it again. With effort, he stilled his breath to hear their words.

"Arat?" Philomene's voice was pleading.

She turned, cheeks wet. "How much to tell—" she paused, wiping her nose with the back of her hand. "It is our greatest challenge you know, deciding how much is right for us to tell. I thought I knew until a moment ago, but options that once stood bright before me are there no longer." Her voice faded as she closed her eyes. "How much to tell?"

Fear shot through the Philomene's eyes, instantly replaced with a look of irritation at the noise of his guards helping Jittan up behind him. A deep moan rose from the soldier as he regained consciousness. Philomene turned to watch them.

Khiron realized the mage felt that his guardsman may have cost them much by his foolishness. If the Arat had been injured, or if she decided to hold back something she would have otherwise shared, that effort could be all for naught.

A sniff brought the mage's focus back to the Arat. Her eyes were red but no longer wet, the wiping of her nose had left a smear of glistening dirt across her lips and cheek. He looked at her with a sense of trepidation; eyes longing for her to speak but afraid of what she might say.

"I am at risk," she said abruptly. "I have foreseen that if I stay here, I will perish, as well as many of the people I love. I also see that I may be killed if I leave, but that future is not certain." A look of fatigue marked her expression as she spoke, but she spoke with authority. "Either way, I must go.

"Tell the Great Raja he needs to send for a Sibulla with haste. By the favor of the Ancients, I perceive that one of their order is visiting the Kingdom of Chalice but will be leaving soon. Send a delegation to the Priory at their Grand Reef. If a ship is sent tomorrow it can be there in time to intercept her, but you must move with haste." She rested a hand on his. "I cannot express it enough, the presence of the Sibulla is pivotal to the future of our kingdom." She turned and started to walk away, then stopped, speaking again without turning. "I see a caramel brown-skinned people." She paused, her eyes tightening. "I don't see clearly concerning them, but I warn you, do your best not to offend them. Remember my words and take note; wisdom is not only reserved for the royal or the aged."

With that, she ran in the direction that the soldiers had come, her short legs moving quickly.

Khiron rose from his hiding place and hastened to their point of rendezvous. She would be safe amongst the villagers and wouldn't have any more problems from the soldiers that he could sense. His mind raced as he processed what he had heard. The tension in his gut was replaced with a cold fire. Nothing would kill her, this he swore.

He increased his pace as he leapt from path to path, with only the moans of Jittan in pursuit.

2
___

RAJA OF CEIDON

"Is that the entirety of what she told you?"

"It is, Great Raja," Philomene said. "Although I'm sure that it is not the full extent of what she saw."

The Raja of the Ceidon, the Brazen Shield of Mount Ceidon and the ruler of the Kingdom of Zaim, grunted. Shifting his heavy frame to face his advisor directly, his eyebrows raised questioningly. "And you say she is a girl of only eleven years?"

"I am sure of it, great Raja."

"Magery? A reborn?"

"No my lord, she bore none of the signs. She is a young girl in truth, although I believe her sight has matured her in ways we can only surmise."

He sighed. "Indulge me."

Philomene's eyes drifted from his liege as he looked off into the distance. "It is said the Arat is a seer. I not only believe that to be true, but I believe she is an anomaly even among those with the sight." He lifted a hand before his face and wiggled his fingers, his eyes coming to rest on his palm. "It is believed seers can see the future, but I was taught at the dojon that such a belief is quite incomplete. Many who have the sight have visions of the future. They usually are limited to an individual who they can focus on, or on events in the near future. We call them seers, and that is technically true, but they are the least of those with the ability." His voice drifted off as he tightened his fingers together as if his hand were a blade. "One stream, one possible future, a vision that is usually accurate, but not always.

"True seers perceive multiple streams of possibility simultaneously, as clearly as they see the unfolding present. That much information would be enough to incapacitate even a seasoned mage with dojon training." He lowered his hand and stood thoughtfully, his head tilted slightly as if looking at something from an unusual angle. Time passed in silence as he stared into the distance.

"Philomene!"

The mage's head snapped erect, eyes once again focusing on his liege. "Many apologies, O Great Raja."

He cleared his throat. "My Lord, the Arat is a true seer. What it must take for her to handle so much information, to discern substance from shadow, to ride the currents and not be destroyed? It's terrifying."

"We all do the same, Philomene." He waved his hand dismissively. "We all dream. We all take in information from many sources, assess it, and make decisions accordingly. What makes you believe this little girl more powerful than us, much less a dojon-trained mage?"

His eyes opened wide. "No, great Raja, I did not mean to imply that she was more powerful than a mage, though she may be. I speak only of the capacity to handle the amount of information she constantly receives."

The Raja of Ceidon's brow furled, his jaw tightening in impatience.

Philomene hurried on. "I speak of inputs, Great Raja. We are used to taking in multiple inputs at a time: sight, sound, smell, and so on. Imagine having all those inputs multiplied by an exponential number of possibilities. What I mean to say is, imagine smelling, seeing, feeling, hearing, and experiencing every stream of the possible future at once. It would be perceptual chaos. To process information from different times, locales, languages, emotional states..." He inhaled deeply then exhaled. "The scope of it beggars the imagination. How does she remain centered in her existential reality amidst such a deluge of possibility?"

"And you believe this about her from meeting her once?" he asked. Doubt was in his inflection.

"From what I've been taught about those with the 'sight,' what I've heard of her previously, and from what she did to Jittan; yes, Great Raja. I do."

The Raja sat thoughtfully, chin resting on finger-tips which were pressed together as if in prayer. He let the moment linger, the slight echo of Philomene's words fading to silence. Slowly his face relaxed, and the flush dissipated, his normal hue returning.

Philomene stood patiently, hands grasped behind the small of his back.

"And you believe she did as she said and left our kingdom, dear counsellor?"

He nodded. "I had one of our spies monitor her movements. She booked passage on a merchant ship heading to—"

"And after all you've said about her, you thought it wise to let her go?" There was an edge in the Raja's voice as he cut off Philomene's answer, his face again darkening.

Philomene's response was low and measured. "Great Raja, as your advisor over the years, I have seen and experienced much. On more than one occasion, you have taught me the value of following one's intuition, weighing probabilities, and trusting the feelings that arise when engaged in the process. The thought did come to me to arrest her, or at least to bar her ability to travel. Yet I ask you, Great Raja, what more could she give us? And with the poignancy of her gift, how would I be able to keep her here beyond her will? Most likely, she would see the multiple lines of future possibility and adjust accordingly. She is loved amongst the commoners," he paused briefly, "not as much as you, Great Raja, but she is loved indeed. In a time that we need unity to defend the kingdom, I didn't feel it beneficial to do anything beyond sharing her words with you."

The Raja sat back on his throne. He looked thoughtful, the signs of anger abating. "I put great trust in your opinion, Philomene. This the entire kingdom knows well. But there is a sizable difference between sharing an opinion for me to consider and making a decision for me." His voice dropped to a whisper as he leaned forward towards his advisor. "In the Ancient Dris' name, never let this happen again."

Philomene bowed deeply, face full of contrition. "As is your will, Great Raja."

"Nothing more will be said of the matter." The Raja sat up and pulled one of three rings hidden on the underside of the right arm of his throne. It was connected to a silk cord that was momentarily visible before returning back to the ornate wooden arm. A long moment passed, and then the gold-inlaid doors that marked the far side of the room opened. An older man entered wearing a silver robe, a tree with hanging fruit stitched in gold on its back. Dark hair with streaks of grey ringed a bald pate, slicked back and ending in a long braid. He entered the round room with his head lowered, passing the alcoves that bracketed the walls with statues of past Rajas without a glance. His bare feet made no sound upon the stone-tiled floor, flowing over the constellations designed in its face like a ghost in the wind. He stopped at the room's center and bowed.

"Master of Swords," the Great Raja said with an even tone, "how fares my guardsman, Jittan?"

Bowing again, he stood, keeping his gaze set towards the floor. "Great Raja, Shield of Ceidon, Master of the Crops that feed the world, he has been disciplined by my hand."

The Raja's eyes grew heavy, knowing the range of what that could mean. "Prepare him for presentation. I will have an audience with him within the hour."

"Great Raja, it has already been done according to your desire. As I knew you had not yet given word about him, I was exceedingly gentle."

The Raja glanced at his advisor briefly before turning back to the tall, sun-kissed man, who stood with his head bowed. "Well done, Master of Swords. Our defenses?"

"Brazen Shield of Ceidon, they are at full readiness and await your command."

A look of appreciation lit across the Raja's face. "Exceptional. Have him brought immediately. I will call for you again soon."

The Master of Swords bowed, turned, and seemed to glide back to the door. As he exited the chamber, there were two quick claps and Jittan appeared, being helped into the room by two of the royal guard.

They struggled with the guardsman, bringing him to the center of the room. Waiting until they were satisfied that he could stand unassisted, the guardsmen released him and left. The door closed without sound, and soon the room was still, Jittan's ragged breathing the only breakage of the silence.

Philomene turned to face Jittan with an air of disdain, but his brows lifted slightly as he took in the state of the man.

The royal guardsman stood unsteadily with a slight bend towards his left. Where his skin was revealed, he was covered in welts, his face, neck, and hands no exception. Swollen and discolored, he looked like a different person.

"Jittan," the Great Raja said coldly, "you have threatened the dominion of our realm. You attacked the warning bell of our kingdom, the Arat, loved by many of my subjects. What do you say to these things?"

Jittan steadied his legs with effort as they had started to shake as the Raja spoke. "It is as you have said, Great Lord." His voice was a raspy whisper as his mouth was swollen shut.

"You were tended to by the healers when you arrived. Why do you stand before me in this state?"

Philomene knew that, like himself, the Raja wanted to know what the Master of Swords had done to the guardsman. Just what did the man consider an 'exceedingly gentle' disciplinary response?

Jittan inhaled deeply as if he was seeking to empty the room of air. Then he spoke.

"The Master of Swords armed me with a training switch, and then himself, and we sparred." His eyes fell. "That was all."

Dris' beard, Philomene thought. *He stands like this from a sparring match where he could defend himself?*

"Training switch," the Raja said as if he had misheard him.

Jittan seemed to shrink where he stood. "Yes, Great Raja. They are in abundance in the training rooms. They are long branches the trainees are tasked to collect that we clean and smooth." A quick inhale. "They bend, but are quite strong." A racking cough took him. He stabilized himself as his legs wobbled momentarily.

A mere branch was used to do this! Despite his anger at the guardsman for what his actions could have cost the kingdom, Philomene's hardness broke, and he began to pity him. His lord didn't seem to share his sentiment.

"I see," the Raja said impassively. "Visit my personal healer immediately and then report to the Master of Swords for your new assignment."

Jittan attempted to bow but ended up just barely nodding his head. The doors opened, and the two guardsmen who had previously supported him came forward, grasped him beneath his shoulders, and escorted him out of the chamber.

The Raja stared at the closed doors as the seconds grew long. "Your thoughts, Philomene?" His tone was curious.

"His body is damaged, but it is his confidence that has been eviscerated. You are wise to reassign him."

"No," he waved his hand dismissively. "What do you feel about our Master of Swords?"

Philomene turned towards the Steep Bay, the long space where the room was exposed to the open air, watching the tops of trees sway in the passing of a wind that didn't reach into the chamber. His thumb rubbed the bottom of his ring lightly as he gazed out into the greater world. "He is a resource that has exceeded my expectations."

He faced the Raja. "When Jakgrim brought him to us as his recommendation to take his place as Master of Swords, I was ambivalent. Jakgrim is dojon-trained, and for him to recommend anyone held much weight, so I supported his request. However, when this proposed Master of Swords stood before us that day, I thought him an obsequious dullard."

The Raja sat, looking at him intently.

"Since then, this master has proven quite brilliant, and my opinion of him couldn't be higher." His brows raised as if in bewilderment. "What we witnessed today reveals not only the efficacy of our Master of Swords but providence in his being here now. The Ancient Dris smiles upon us, O Brazen Shield of Ceidon. Such talent we have not seen within our borders before, and Dris knows, we now need it."

"As well as a Sibulla you say," the Raja quipped, eyes still sharp upon him.

"Beyond any doubt, Great Raja."

The Raja leaned forward with concern in his eyes. "You have been my trusted advisor for some time now, and even a friend. You understand that there is no need for you to feel as if you have to protect your position, even regarding an eleven-year-old seer with special sight. This you know, yes?"

Philomene fought the urge to remonstrate. The thought of the Arat supplanting him had never entered his mind, but he saw no benefit in making the argument. The Raja's views were what they were, and his explanation would only serve to lend validity to what his leader already believed. "Thank you, Great Raja. I am ever honored to be in your service, and shall do so with joy until the Ancient Nihil comes to collect my cold flesh."

The Raja's gaze softened. "I am pleased." He pulled the far right ring beneath his throne's arm, and a golden cord became visible. In moments the great doors opened, and a woman wearing a decorative leather light armor entered.

"My Lord Raja," she said. Her hair was braided and wrapped in a tight bun. "Your command?"

"Prepare to leave within the hour on the Crest. The ship must leave for the shores of Chalice as soon as you embark. You will find a Sibulla at the Priory just off of the Grand Reef. Bring her here with urgency. Two swordsmen will await you onboard. And Rephna," he paused, "nothing must impede you in this mission."

She nodded her understanding.

The Raja turned to his advisor, and Philomene took a ring from his pocket bearing the Raja's personal seal and handed it to her. "Give this to the Sibulla when you find her. It says all that she will need to hear."

Rephna took the ring, bowed, and left the chamber.

As the doors closed and the weight of the room's silence returned, the Raja reclined and turned to look through the Steep Bay. "Philomene, I hope your faith in the Arat is well placed, or that she is an utter charlatan, and no war with the Ulaan is imminent. I have placed our kingdom on the scales of honor and dishonor, all on the word of an eleven-year-old child."

Philomene gazed out through the Steep Bay with his ruler. He gazed and said not a word.

3

NNESUTEE

They sat within the hold of the merchant ship, the sailors, and their captain hard at work top-side. Khiron watched as the Arat played with two other girls near her age, the round rocks she had brought rolling around the floor as the ship made its way through choppy waves. Their giggles and laughter made bearable the dread cold that seemed to seep from every wooden plank.

Seven passengers shared the hold with him and the Arat.

A family of four, two of which were the Arat's play-mates. The mother, for the children's resemblance to her was undeniable, was attractive. She was chubby with a natural smile and looked to be quite strong as she had moved a few of the loaded crates with her husband earlier to make more room for them to sleep.

The husband was as pale as the bleached nets that gave cover to some of the kingdom's crops. A smaller man, he looked to have known a life of hard work hidden from sunlight. It was likely the motion of the ship, and not some malady, that caused him to look in such a state.

Further down the starboard side, closer to the aft, was someone laying on the floor wrapped in brown cloaks which wholly obscured the person's face. No straw or cushion was beneath the prone form. Only the occasional rise and fall of the fabric marked that they weren't sharing the hold with a corpse. Still, he had seen no other movement from that direction for a few hours now.

Sitting on the port side down from him were a woman and man, who looked to be veteran sell-swords or mercenaries. The woman sharpened her sword while the man whittled away at a block of wood with a curved knife. The rectangular tattoos that lined their left cheeks, which stretched from beneath their eyes to their jawline, said they were not native to any kingdom within the hemisphere. They kept to themselves and had spent the previous hour engaging in strange stretching exercises.

The ship had pulled into port the night before to unload and load shipments. With the morning tide, they had set off to what he now knew was the port city of Chalice, on the Northwest Coast of the continent of

Bacileisa. With the exception of the family, the others had come from the ship's previous stops.

Wonders had been spoken about Chalice, its outer wall made of a mysterious rounded crystal that darkened at odd times of the day. A visitor to Zaim years ago said the wall of Chalice was smooth to the touch and that it stood six times the height of the average swordsman, even when wearing their boots. He chuckled inwardly at the memory. Rumored to be unbreakable, the wall is what had given the city its name.

Magery was commonplace within its borders, and it was one of few kingdoms he knew of that boasted an active Arch Mage. Despite himself, he was excited that he was going to be able to see it.

"That your daughter?"

Torn from his thoughts, he turned. It was the male sell-sword who had spoken.

"Close," he replied with a raspy voice. He cleared his throat.

"How'd she get those?" The sell-sword tilted his knife towards the round rocks which continually rolled and changed directions between the girls.

"Baubles from the mainland," Khiron grinned. "It's rare to find them so round. I thought she would like them, but I didn't realize they would be this much fun for her. They have been a pleasant distraction from the rigors of the journey."

The sell-sword went back to whittling, wood chips and shavings collecting between his feet. "Interesting that casting stones would be just laying around on their lonesome."

"Casting stones?"

The female sell-sword looked up. "Who is the girl, swordsman? We mean you no harm."

The Arat turned to them from playing, her missing-toothed smile wide as she pushed a rock against the pull of the ship's lean. She glanced at Khiron and gave the slightest of nods.

He frowned, leaning into the hilt of his sword for its comfort. "My niece. She has a knack for predicting things. She is young but is right more times than not. Why do you ask?"

Neither sell-sword responded, going back to what they were doing as if nothing had been said.

Khiron stayed on alert for a while, but nothing untoward happened. Time droned on as the girls played, their laughter free and unrestrained, and slowly he relaxed.

As the day passed, the girls were called back by their parents to eat, and the Arat came and sat beside Khiron.

"I'm hungry," she said, a frown forming on her face.

He grunted with a wide smile. "I thought you'd forgotten about eating for a while there. Here." He unrolled some bread and cheese, and unstoppered a flask of water and handed it to her.

They ate in relative silence. She burped and then giggled. "Excuse me." The look on her face was as silly as he had seen.

She was making this journey easier for him. He hated ships, and the idea of traveling in a cargo hold hadn't made the idea more palatable. Yet here he sat, back hurting, joints aching, and grinning like a child.

"Little girl," the male sell-sword said, breaking into their laughter. "This is for you."

Khiron pushed his sword away from his side a little, loosening it about an inch from its scabbard, grin gone. *Dris' beard! I knew this was too good to last.*

The sell-sword held up a wooden figurine. It was the Arat, the detail precise, even down to her missing tooth. His grin was humorless, and his eyes cold. "Thought you might like this as a memento of your journey."

Khiron started to rise, but the Arat put her hand upon his leg and squeezed, sending him the message to stand down.

He wanted to scream, to throw off her hand and draw his sword and cut down these sell-swords where they sat, but he did nothing. A look of thanks held in the Arat's eyes.

Across the hold, the parents of the girls pulled

them closer. The mother yanked something from her boot and placed it beneath her worn cloak.

"My arm is getting tired," the sell-sword said in an entreating tone. "Won't you take this from me?" He leaned in their direction, a mere dozen steps away.

The female sell-sword dropped her sharpening stone and lifted her blade. "You ungrateful brat. Would you rather have this?" She shifted her sword back and forth. "Or this," she drew a curved dagger from a leg sheath, standing and then taking a martial stance.

The Arat kept her hand on Khiron. She looked not in the least concerned.

"So you threaten children now?" a fatigued voice said from further back in the hold. "When did Atiere hunters threaten little girls, regardless of what power you may sense from them?"

Both sell-swords turned to face the one who spoke with swords raised, and then with eyes wide with fear, lowered their weapons and abased themselves.

The figure who spoke was the person who had lain beneath the cloaks. Now standing, he cut an imposing figure. He was taller than all of them by a head's height or more. Brown-skinned and ageless, he had a face with a broad forehead that cut to a narrow chin. Wide, developed shoulders anchored a long neck, and his body seemed to be lean, developed muscle beneath his wrinkled clothes. He held a wooden walking staff, which from the floor, came to just under his chin.

What stuck Khiron more than anything was the man's eyes. They were large, almond-shaped, and were a milky white. *By Dris' hoary beard, the man is blind!*

His movements were smooth as he moved toward Khiron and the Arat, passing the almost cowering Atiere hunters. He stopped at the sound of the figurine sliding as the ship shifted. Reaching down, he picked it up gently. "I think this gift should not go to waste." He came two paces from them before sitting before them. "Now, that is better."

The Arat's giggle seemed entirely out of place, yet it stole the threat from the air. Even the girls cowering in their parent's arms lifted their faces from the folds of their cloaks to peer out.

"You are one of the Nnesutee aren't you?" The Arat's question was filled with fascination. "The tribe of nomads born from the union of royals of the empire of—"

His hand rose sharply. "Say not the name. They have remained quiet in this dimension for almost an age. You speaking their name now would draw attention, despite us being on the open waters, and would put the lives of everyone on this vessel in jeopardy."

Her mouth clamped shut, and she looked apologetically at Khiron, whose hand had been on the grip of his sword since the man stood up.

"The Atiere hunters sensed your power, yet I sense it is easy for you, young seer." He grinned. "Unfathomable depths are easily plumbed by one who is born within them. Only those who have been set apart by nature can understand." He motioned towards some fruit, and Khiron tossed it to him, forgetting that the man was blind. Moving quicker than could be reacted to, the man unsheathed and re-sheathed a hidden sword in his walking staff. The red fruit was sliced in four equal parts, collecting in his hands as they fell.

Khiron's mouth fell open, as probably did everyone's in the cargo hold. He carefully moved his hand away from his sword's hilt.

"Thank you," the Nnesutee said, taking a bite of one of the parts. "Would you like a slice?"

The Arat giggled incessantly, and, strangely enough, the man joined in.

Khiron didn't see the humor in any of it.

4

A PASSING GLANCE

Bright light flooded the cargo hold as a crewman of the merchant ship looked in. "We sighted de land, and we be at port in a less dan an hour." His voice was a raspy gravel, the stench of rotting teeth filling the hold. "Cap'n says keep quiet, and be ready da move quick when de time comes." He cleared his throat, spat where fortunately they couldn't see, and closed the hatch.

It took a few seconds for their eyes to adjust to the returning dimness, then everyone began to pack their things. They were finished packing in less than a minute.

The girls hadn't played with the Arat since the Atiere hunters had caused the disruption. With the blind Nnesutee now awake and sitting with Khiron and the Arat, neither the Atiere hunters nor the family spoke. They all kept a wary distance from the group and looked to be attempting to be as invisible as possible.

Khiron was surprised that he was able to sleep last night. The Arat had slept shortly after their meal, and the Nnesutee had sat head bowed as if in meditation. The man had still been in that meditative pose when he slipped into sleep.

They had slept long, over ten hours in a cold and uncomfortable space. It was unnatural. He wondered if the Arat had anything to do with that, or was it the Nnesutee in some way.

Khiron had woken about ten minutes before the crewman made his announcement. When he looked at the family on the other side of the hold, they didn't seem to have been awake long either.

The Arat wiped her eyes with the back of her hand and yawned. She reached into their pack and pulled out some fruit and cheese, giving some to him and then to the Nnesutee. She spoke quietly to the blind swordsman between chewing with a mouth full of grapes. "They could have used you back in Zaim. They still can. Someone of your skill would be a help against the Ulaan."

A sad grin formed on the Nnesutee's face. "Young seer, you cannot see everything, and when it comes to my kind and my forebears, you see little at all."

The Arat sat attentively at that, chin lifting with eyes wide.

As the silence continued, the Nnesutee sighed. "The Ulaan soldiers are dojon-rated masterful swordsmen who worship the Ancient Dris. Although Dris is often called the Ancient of War, in truth, he is the Ancient of Swordsmanship. In a clash with such swordsmen, my presence would not make much of a difference. As it is, one of my tribe is already serving in the royal palace."

Khiron stuttered in reply. "One of you? Serving? Who? Where?"

"Not now, Khiron," the Arat said. "Forgive us. Please, I need to understand."

The Nnesutee nodded. "The first dojon recorded was formed by Master Swordsman Raphon, the swordsmaster of the First Age. He formed the dojon and its systems from what he learned from the Ancient Dris. The system that rates and ranks both swordsmen and mages in the span of the unified dimensions comes from him. The Ulaan soldiers are gifted swordsmen. Their code stipulates that one has to reach at least a 'masterful swordsman' ranking to qualify for their swordsmen corp."

"I didn't know swordsmen were ranked," Khiron said, not able to hold his thought. "I know of dojons, and trained for two years with a dojon-trained swordsman, but I have never heard of this."

She didn't rebuke him.

"It is known by those who trained in one," the Nnesutee replied, "and all dojons are not equal. Official dojons hold to a strict discipline that can take years of study. They are centered on Raphon's philosophy of currents, balance, and values. The system is based on an ontological study that touches the mind, the body, and consciousness itself."

The Arat tilted forward slightly, her eyes a fount of concentration. In the time he'd known her, Khiron had never seen her so focused. It seemed to him that things were falling into place for her, missing pieces of information that limited her interpretation of what she saw. She seemed to be solidifying before him, becoming more of who she was in the span of the Nnesutee's words. A part of him rejoiced at her revelation, and yet another part mourned. It should've been a good thing, but he couldn't shake the feeling of loss. He was her sworn-sword, but he had begun to feel like a parent, or at least what he thought a parent should feel. In his service to her, she had been both prophet and child, and the latter seemed to be fading.

"The rating system used at dojons is based on Raphon's understanding of balance as the ideal state of all things physical, psychological, and cosmic. It posits that all species, races, and powers are necessary for balance and seeks to cause inter-dimensional balance by creating balance in each being and aspected power.

The rating system establishes the ideal state of each practitioner. It then marks where they are in relation to that ideal."

"Then those who follow the disciplines of the dojon are worshippers of the Ancient Me'ett," the Arat said.

He chuckled. "I can see how you would come to that conclusion. As the Ancient of Balance, the Ancient Me'ett would seem the logical choice. Yet, if one looks from a different perspective, all of the Ancients and their aspects are about balance." He rubbed his chin. "One does not need to worship an Ancient to train in a dojon, nor give them fealty as if they were their lord." His grin flashed a row of pearly white teeth. "My forebears believed in the presence of the Ancients but did not worship them in the least. They believed in a higher power—" His voice faded off into silence, his milky eyes looking somehow more distant. He lowered his head towards the Arat, his face a solemn mask. "My forebears believed a dojon's purpose was not to master anything greater than the self. They mastered all the dojon could offer and then declared it insufficient in that cause."

"So dojons are flawed?" Khiron asked with a hint of incredulity.

The Nnesutee's grin returned as he lifted his head to face the sworn-sword. "So my forebears believed—"

"And yet believe," finished the Arat.

The Nnesutee's grin bloomed into a verdant smile. "Indeed, they believe it still." He leaned back and stretched, his chin moving from one side, then the other, before he straightened and leaned on his staff, which he grasped with both hands, standing.

"I believe I know who your forebears were." The Arat spoke like a child who had learned a secret, her voice lowering as she continued. "They are not only a name heard in a whisper from the past, but I know who and where they are in the present."

The Nnesutee inclined his head in her direction, bringing his mouth beside her ear. "Where you have been heading all along—"

Her clap was so sudden that Khiron jumped. "Hah!" she exclaimed with unfeigned joy, "I knew it!"

"Knew what?" Khiron asked in earnest. She didn't pause.

"But wait," she said. "What can I do to ensure that they come?"

The Nnesutee pulled up the cowls of both cloaks above his head. "What do seers do, young one? They see. What greater gift for a seer than to see the future unfold with her own eyes." With that, he rose and walked back to the place where he had lain when they had embarked, the Atiere hunters abasing themselves as he passed.

Arriving at the port, they disembarked with stiff limbs and aching joints. Even the children were the worse for wear. Led down the jetty by a scrawny sailor with large forearms, most of them squinting and covering their eyes from the sudden light of the twin suns that stood high. The heat was a great relief from the cold they experienced in the merchant ship, and everyone stretched and smiled as the cold lifted from them.

They separated quickly, the Atiere hunters heading south of the city with speed, and the children from the family waving before approaching a carriage.

Behind them, the Nnesutee was being escorted down by the Captain himself. "There is a road before you. If you walk about seventy steps in a straight line, there is a row of carriages, and any of them will take you where you want to go. Tell them you are a guest of the Captain of the Old Crate, and you will not have to pay a thing."

"Thank you, Captain. Your generosity exceeds my ability to express the gratitude I feel."

"Sir, with you aboard, we had the quickest runs to the ports at the Isle of Ivory, Zaim, Laor, and now Chalice. Traditionally, this run should have taken a half-day longer. We sailors are often considered a superstitious bunch. I've seen a lot in my forty-one years piloting the waves, and never once have I seen a run like this. You are a sailor's charm, sir, and I am honored to have served you. If ever we meet again, you will have my cabin as your own. Are you sure I can't walk you to the carriage?"

"I am sure, Captain. Thank you for such kind words. Please don't let me hinder your unloading or allow me to eat away any more of the excellent time you made on this trip." With that, he nodded, and using his staff, walked towards the Arat and Khiron. The captain stared after him with a grin before turning to bark orders to his crew.

"I sense that you are unique, even amongst the Nnesutee," she said as he reached them.

"That I may be. We are all unique in our little ways, we humans. It is what makes us worth saving." He started walking down the wooden path to the carriage stand.

She looked confused for a moment and then called after him. "May I ask one more question before you go?"

"Of course, young seer."

"You are heavily obscured, but even so, I sense that you are a skilled swordsman and a mage of considerable power," she said. Her eyes were full, but there was a serious set to her mouth.

"Your question?"

"If your fellow Nnesutee is serving the Raja of Ceidon, can't he join with Philomene the Guileless, and they use their joined power to eradicate the threat?"

"You can't see much about our tribe, young seer, but you can about the Ulaan. What do you see that stands out beyond their martial ability?"

She stood still, her eyes focused as she concentrated, then puffed. "Their ability is great, although I only sense a few that have your strength. But I do see that none of them use magery, as if there is not a mage amongst them."

"There is not, but you yet miss what you seek. Remember, young seer, beyond what you see with your natural senses, and beyond what you see with your gifts, you must always trust your heart. Your spirit knows what your mind does not. It sees what you will overlook. Trust your heart." He turned and left them without another word, making his way to the carriages, extending his staff in a side-to-side motion before him as walked the path.

The Arat and Khiron watched him speak to a driver and enter his carriage before they began to walk towards Chalice. They barely traveled fifty paces before she changed direction, leading them up the coast.

"Where are we going?" Khiron asked. His body ached, he was tired and wasn't in the mood for a side trip.

"On another ship, of course. This is not our destination."

"But, we just arrived here!" Khiron realized that he

sounded like the child, and she the adult. It soured his mood, but he was determined to get some warm food and rest. "When do we need to be where we are heading?"

Her eyes tightened for a moment as if looking into the distance, then relaxed. "Two days at the latest."

"How long will it take us to make the journey?"

She frowned. "A day at best."

"And how are we paying for this trip?"

She looked bashful for the first time since he had known her. "With the money pouch I lifted from Philomene the Guileless?" She looked up and to the sides, avoiding his eyes.

"No, you don't. Look at me." He waited. "Now, when did you take his money pouch?"

She bit her lip and then broke into a grin. "Directly after I hit his guardsman. It was almost in the same move. I thought it a thing of beauty."

He stared at her sternly, then started to grin himself. "So, how much is in there?"

"Oh, enough to eat, get new clothes, sleep at an Inn, and book a ship to take us where we need to go... and maybe just a little more than that." She winked.

"Who would have thought that the Arat was—"

"What? A girl who takes care of her protector? Why, yes. Yes, I am." She jingled her bag of casting stones in one hand, and a full money pouch in the other.

"Where did you keep it?"

"Close to where we sat. It was in plain sight the entire trip."

"I didn't see it!"

"And now you know the reason I kept it there."

He searched his memory, but for the life of him, he couldn't remember seeing it anywhere.

"Now," she said in a mocking voice, "take me to Chalice. We need to eat and to rest."

He started to protest until he realized what she had said. Turning with a smile, he ran towards a carriage that had just stopped, passengers climbing out stretching their limbs.

The Arat turned abruptly to see two women in the distance walking onto a private jetty followed by two swordsmen carrying a large chest. They walked with an air of dignity onto a sleek ship, its sails lifting and oars hovering just above the low waves.

One woman was in light armor, her hair tied into a bun. The other was a woman with an ageless face whose every feature and movement was a thing of grace. She wore a grey dress with split sides revealing matching trousers beneath. Her sleeves were long, and she wore tight gloves of the same color. Her braided hair stretched to the small of her back, and even from a distance, her eyes held power.

The woman in grey turned and caught her gaze. They stared at each other for a long breath before the woman in light armor came and motioned for her to follow. The woman in grey gave a brief nod of recognition and entered the ship with her host. It was only then that the Arat heard Khiron hailing her. He had booked the carriage.

She sprinted, hair flying back and arms outstretched as if she was a flying bird, and stopped abruptly. A look of sheer terror was on her face when Khiron reached her.

"What? What is it? Are you all right?" His questions were panicked.

She shook her hands as if trying to cool herself off, her words rushing out between breaths. "Khiron! I see what I missed; what the Nnesutee wanted me to see on my own. Oh, what a fool I've been not to see it sooner."

Khiron held her shoulders and looked at her. "What? What is it?"

She regained control of herself. The suddenness of her transformation from eleven-year-old excitement to cold detatchment chilled him.

"It matters not," she said blandly. "Nothing that we can do about it now anyway. I'm hungry. Let's get something to eat." Without a backward look, she walked up to the carriage and climbed in, leaving a concerned Khiron frozen where he stood.

5

SIBULLA

A golden scaled dragon flew high above Mount Ceidon, heading north into the unknown. The Raja of Ceidon and Philomene the Guileless watched it diminish into the distance through the Steep Bay, both standing near its stone ledge.

"A fell portent, Philomene?"

"It was a golden dragon, and that bodes well, Great Raja. They have never been the enemy of humankind."

"So you have said before. I should have remembered your words."

"No, Great Raja. Your sagacious perceptions and willingness to make difficult decisions are the mortar that holds this kingdom together. Let it never be said that you ask too few questions, my lord."

The Raja looked fatigued. "I am suspending the

rules of protocol, Philomene. This morning, there is no title between us that is higher than 'friend.'" He looked into the distance where the dragon was a mere speck on a tapestry of blue and white. "I've never seen one fly so quickly."

Philomene looked long before turning from the open view. "Neither have I. Then again, I haven't seen many dragons over the span of my life. I have seen them in battle once, and that was once too many."

The Raja watched until the dragon was no longer visible, then turned. His steps were that of a man burdened, the heaviness in each obvious. They had not been so when they had walked to the Steep Bay together minutes before. "I feel a weight I have not felt before, Philomene. I sense a threat that supersedes even that presented by the Ulaan. We may win this battle and still lose everything despite our victory."

"You continue to surprise me, Great…my friend. You are more aware of the flow of reality than most will ever be. You may not be a mage, nor a swordsman, but as a lord, you have few equals."

"It is good for you to say so. I am tired. I have no one I can talk to without the trappings of my office constraining me. I am the Raja of Ceidon, but I am also simply a human. Since Jakgrim left the palace, I have had no one I can bare my thoughts to without weakening our kingdom. A leader's unfiltered thoughts can destroy the grand illusion which makes all of us who rule effective. It is a heavy burden."

Philomene stood silent. He had never thought of the Raja outside of his role as ruler of the kingdom. Over the years that he had served him, his constant thought was for the well-being of the Raja and the kingdom of Zaim. His advice had always been guided with that in mind. He suddenly realized that his time in the dojon in Chalice in his youth had changed him. In his continuing quest to learn more about magery and the depth of its mysteries, he had lost the need for human interaction on a friendship level, or so he believed. What his Raja needed him to be, he wasn't sure he could fulfill. The thought shook him.

The Raja sat back upon the throne as if he had seen twice his years. He didn't speak, keeping his thoughts to himself, his eyes needy as he looked into the distance.

The silence stretched.

Philomene struggled to find what to say. This was an opportunity not given to many: the ability to speak without protocol, to be free to share without worry of offense. To listen to the innermost thoughts of the man who governed the lives of so many thousands. As the Raja's advisor, he knew his role, but as his friend, he was as lost as a leaf in the breeze. Yet his Raja needed him, and he would stand up to the challenge, even if he had no idea how to.

He opened his mouth to speak when a bell sounded. The doors of the throne room opened, and Rephna entered with a Sibulla. Philomene turned to see the Raja's face with no trace of the weight it bore just seconds ago. He felt a pang of sadness. The moment had passed.

"Great Raja of Ceidon, I introduce to you the Sibulla, Zatrin Bei."

"Thank you, Rephna. You may leave us now."

Rephna bowed her head and left the room, the doors closing silently behind her.

"I recognize the role of the Sibulla as the Arbiter of Kingdoms, and hereby grant her equal status according to her station," the Raja said in the formal fashion.

"Thank you," she said with a nod. "It seems that you are on the brink of war."

"I believe so, Arbiter."

"And this is?" she motioned towards Philomene.

"My royal advisor, Philomene the Guileless."

She looked thoughtful, as if scanning through her memories. "Why yes, I know who you are, the mage who fought at Wolf Pass in the midlands of Bacileisa."

"That was a long time ago, but yes, I am he."

"It was quite a long time ago. Do you use the ritual of J'kbar to maintain your vigor? You should look much older."

"No, Arbiter. I did not attain the rank of 'Master' in my discipline."

The Raja's brow raised in ignorance at the terms and span of the conversation. "None of this is pertinent to the cause at hand," he said with thinly veiled irritation. "The Ulaan plan to conquer Zaim, and presumably they will do so by attacking Mount Ceidon directly. We have made preparations to defend the mountain plateau upon which we and all of our visitors stand, but my primary concern is for the hundreds of acres of crops that surround Mount Ceidon. More importantly, the thousands upon thousands of people who call the crops and the areas surrounding them their home. Our army is small, and our mages are few.

"Being on a peninsula with reefs bordering most of our shores has kept us from many issues from the sea. That natural deterrent has been helped even more by Chalice being so close to us. No navy wants to attract their attention, for they just may consider such a force in such close proximity to their shores cause enough for them to respond. Not many can deal with a High Mage.

"We have a pact with Pehnah, the City of Paths, which abuts our western border, but they will not rise against the Ulaan kingdom. No one on this continent will. Not many of the kingdoms of Gaia would. We have ascertained that will be their point of entry."

The Sibulla didn't look impressed. "The size of your army?"

"Approximately five thousand swordsmen and a thousand archers, with a mage corps of seven, led by my advisor, Philomene."

"I see," the Sibulla said. "How far out are the Ulaan? What are their latest movements, and where are your scout reports?"

Philomene shifted uneasily, but the Raja spoke plainly. "We have had no sightings as of yet, nor reports that speak of their whereabouts currently."

"Your signet ring portended an impending attack." Her voice was a mixture of inquisitiveness and rebuke. "What was the source of that information?"

The Raja didn't hesitate. "From the Arat, a seer of great power."

"Where is this seer? I would hear their vision."

"She has left Zaim, Arbiter. She left by ship after sharing her vision."

"You mean to say that I was summoned here and brought from the priory in Chalice on the words of this so-called se—," she lifted a gloved hand as recognition sparked in her eyes. "What did she say precisely?"

At a nod from the Raja, Philomene repeated all she had said verbatim, including the story of their meeting, but leaving out the part of what Jittan had done and her belief of the dangers she was in personally.

"I see. I'm not aware of what kingdom she spoke

of," the Arbiter said. "We Sibulla maintain a living history of the kingdoms that we have had interaction with. Many kingdoms have people with a variety of shades of brown skin, most of which are located on our home continent of Karitichus. Yet, none have the description of power that she seems to have implied."

"That is all we know, Arbiter."

"I understand. Who commands your defenses?"

"Our Master of Swords."

"Thank you, Great Raja. I know that you are not used to being spoken to so directly, but time leaves me no alternative."

"In some ways, Arbiter, it is refreshing."

She smiled at that. "I need to know what your Master of Swords has planned. Pulling up the platforms and lifts that lead up the side of this mountain could hold off many forces indefinitely. Still, the plan to defend the greater part of the kingdom will be important to know."

The Raja pulled a ring beneath his throne's arm while the Sibulla spoke, and as she finished, the doors opened, admitting the Master of Swords.

He entered as before, his bare feet seemingly gliding across the ornate floor. He acknowledged the Sibulla with a deferential nod as he stood beside her and bowed deeply before the Raja, keeping his gaze downward when he rose.

"Look at me, Master of Swords. You have the same liberty to speak before me that my advisor does."

His head slowly lifted until his almond-shaped eyes looked directly into the Raja's own. His gaze was piercing, his face smooth with an aged scar on the right edge of his chin. "I obey as you command, Great Raja."

The Sibulla took close note of him, her eyes seeming to consume every detail. "You are of the Nnesutee are you not? When do the rootless ever take root?"

The Nnesutee's expression was unmoved as his gaze rested on her. "When the soil is rich enough to feed it."

"Rich as in financial gain, Nnesutee?"

"Abundant in its capacity to nurture life, Sibulla. What is the abundance of coin in relation to the bourgeoning breath of a flower? What are the rewards of a blade in relation to the life that one fruit can support? From a single apple, a continent can be fed. As long as one eats only of its flesh and does not consume the seeds, the dimensions can be fed indefinitely."

Philomene started to interrupt the two, but the Raja motioned for him to be silent.

"So you are a seed that has found rich soil?" she asked.

"I am a farmer that prepares the soil for the seeds it will nurture."

She looked at him silently for some time. Both of them locked eyes with neither giving quarter.

Her brow lifted with an air of respect given. "What is your plan of defense, Master of Swords?"

"It rests on the fact that they are worshippers of Dris."

"As is the kingdom of Zaim," she retorted.

"And that is where we have the advantage, Arbiter. The Ulaan teach a strict interpretation in their dojon, and that interpretation governs every aspect of their strategy. According to their teachings, one swordsman can challenge another to single combat. In such a contest, the winner takes all. By this teaching, wars can be fought not only with armies but within a single duel."

"That is the rule of Kath, the arena of the Ancients, Master of Swords. It is where the terms 'First Sword' and 'Sword of the Kingdom' come from, where kingdoms send a solitary swordsman or mage to represent it in combat. It is not the rule beyond its borders."

"What you have said is true, Arbiter, but not when both kingdoms are worshippers of the Ancient Dris. As both we and the Ulaan claim Dris as our Ancient, we fall under the rules of the Dojon of Dris. That rule states that when conflict arises within the faith, a swordsman or mage can be chosen from each opposing perspective to settle the matter through martial prowess. Amongst kingdoms, this also applies.

Dris holds that just as the ruler of a kingdom is the embodiment of their kingdom, and when a ruler concedes to another kingdom, the ruler's kingdom is sundered, so a swordsman can represent a kingdom, with like result."

The Sibulla's lips remained neutral, but there was a grin in her eyes. "As you say, Master of Swords. The Ulaan would only attack this peninsula to control its crops. To ensure that the crops and those who tend them remain healthy, they would most likely not attack the populace, but only those on Mount Ceidon. According to their history, they should attack with a force of between fifteen and fifty. Fifteen dojon-trained swordsmen could cut through a hundred non-dojon trained swordsmen easily. Being that these are Ulaan swordsman, we could safely multiply that number to a few hundred. They would cut down soldiers, swordsmen, and anyone who attacked them or drew a weapon."

The Nnesutee nodded. "I agree with your assessment, Arbiter. Even if all of our swordsmen were on the Mount, once a sufficient number of Ulaan were on the deck, it would make no difference. Accordingly, I have the bulk of our swordsmen doing patrols amongst the crops and communities on the ground, including our most talented swordsmen and archers. We have a token force of swordsmen stationed on the Mount, led by a former royal guardsman. All our mages, with the exception of our royal advisor, are in the spire towers that make up the crown of the palace. With four of the five towers occupied, each mage has two archers assigned to them. We should have ample warning before the Ulaan make it to the palace, giving us time to extend the challenge, which in effect will end the hostilities."

"Your plan of defense is solid, Master of Swords, yet some will be killed in their initial attack."

"Despite our best efforts, the Ulaan will not be defeated without the spilling of blood," he said solemnly. "If any Ancient were to supplant the Ulaan's worship of Dris, it would have to be the Ancient Nihil. The Ulaan are a blood-thirsty people, and Nihil's Wolf is never far from where they tread. But we will minimize the loss of life, and in the process, protect the life of our Raja."

The Sibulla looked satisfied. "What do you perceive as my role in this?"

The Nnesutee bowed before her deeply and rose, showing great deference. "You will be needed to extend the challenge, which will make it legally binding in the eyes of any kingdom who learns of it."

"And who will become the representative Sword of Zaim?"

He bowed again, "why its Master of Swords, of course."

She started to speak when a sound like a thunderclap caused all of them to jump, the explosion followed by an exhalation like a rushing wind. A mephitic odor rushed into the room. Magery.

"So soon?" the Raja exclaimed. "The Ulaan are here so soon?"

"That was from our mage corps, Great Raja. We are under attack!"

The Master of Swords turned and glided towards the door with haste. "Please come, Arbiter. Our moment has arrived."

THE RAJA SAT on his throne, with a look of deep irritation. The explosions had stopped minutes ago, and the silence that followed was almost a physical discomfort. The tension in the air was palpable.

Philomene struggled to hold his composure. Shifting his weight from one leg to the other, he felt as if he had been punched in the stomach. Had the Sibulla been successful? His mages? His heart leapt as the door swung open.

Rephna entered the throne room, her breaths were deep and quick. "My Lord— The battle is finished." She wiped her forehead with the back of her hand and took a moment to gather her breath. "The Ulaan came over the lip of the Mount in rows, one after the other: no shields, just swords. They seemed relaxed as they moved. I saw no panic or concern from any of them. Unless someone unsheathed a weapon, they paid them no mind. Most people either ran or abased themselves."

Philomene cleared his throat. "Our swordsmen? Mages?"

Her face reddened. "They struck our swordsmen down with ease. Everyone I saw who drew a weapon against them was in Nihil's grasp before they could use it. The air of nonchalance in their movements was... chilling." She looked into Philomene's eyes, and her gaze fell. "A small detachment of Ulaan broke from their formation and scaled the towers toward the mages. They arrived as the Sibulla presented herself. I turned to report when she reached them. That is all I know."

Philomene's brow lined in concern.

"Dris bless you, Rephna," the Raja said, his voice steady. "That will be all."

She bowed then walked to the doors, pausing the length of a long sigh, then left the throne room.

Black smoke rose past the Steep Bay in curling wisps, a smell both acrid and sweet filled the chamber. Occasionally, the sound of voices reached the throne room, but none of them were decipherable.

The great Raja toyed with the rings beneath the throne's arm, sliding his fingers across each one.

Philomene, stood stiffly, continually rubbing his hands together.

Finally, a bell rang, and the doors of the throne room opened. The Sibulla entered first, followed by the Master of Swords and three Ulaan. The first two were tall women, and the last was a male of average height, their skin color split down the center of their faces: one-half pale blue, the other a soft gold. They wore tanned leather armor and carried two swords: one across their backs, and the other at their sides. It was the first time Philomene could remember a weapon being in the throne room other than the Raja's sword. Neither the Sibulla nor the Master of Swords was armed.

The Sibulla took a position between the Raja and the Ulaan swordsmen, the Master of Swords coming to stand a step behind her on her left side.

"Great Raja of Ceidon, Brazen Shield of Mount Ceidon, and ruler of the Kingdom of Zaim, I present to you UiNemtasma, the leader of this delegation," she said. Uilia, her Second, and Uinni," moving a hand before each as she introduced them. She then spoke to the Ulaan in their own tongue, a musical language that was smooth and flowed like honey from the tongue.

"We do not need translation," UiNemtasma said. Her eyes burned brightly framed between her braided straight hair. "We speak the Zaim tongue, as well as the tongue of every kingdom that worships the Ancient of the Sword."

"Very well. You understand the honor of royal title. As none of you are one of the Ruling Nine, you must direct all your comments to me when speaking to the Raja of Mount Ceidon."

"Acceptable," UiNemtasma said. "I recognize the role of the Sibulla as the Arbiter of Kingdoms, and hereby grant her equal status according to her station."

The Sibulla nodded her acceptance of the declaration, as did the Raja.

"I am the highest-ranked of the Ulaan present, and as I have accepted the challenge, I will speak for our kingdom. As you have said, I would have Uilia as my witness and second and will send Uinni to lead our—," she paused as she searched for a word,"—delegation beyond your borders."

Uinni bowed and moved without pause to the doors, which began to open just as he arrived before them. He slipped through the still opening doors and was gone.

The Raja spoke. "What are the casualties?"

The Sibulla remained silent, indicating that the question was directed to the Master of Swords.

"We lost all of the swordsmen on the Mount that were not within the palace, Great Raja. We also lost three of the mages along with their archers. Of those of the guard on the Mount who were not in the palace proper, only two archers survived. As of the last report, we lost none of our number that were not on the mount.'

The Raja was a mask of calm, but Philomene thought he saw a slight look of discomfort in his gaze. What it meant he would have to ask later. As it was, it had been so quick that he may have imagined it.

"Did we have any civilian casualties?"

"One, Great Raja," he said. "A woman visiting the Mount who has been here for eight days. Her registration at the Royal Inn says she is a scholar from the island kingdom of Zuutin. She had many samples of soil from different parts of our gardens wrapped in paper rolls in her room. We also found notes in a language we thus far have not been able to translate. The notes are extensive."

"I am not familiar with this kingdom," the Raja said.

"Neither am I, my lord," the master of swords said with an unusual concern.

"UiNemtasma," the Raja said, "why was this woman killed?"

The Sibulla repeated the question to the Ulaan swordsman in a neutral tone.

"She drew a sword when we crested the Mount and flooded the city. She was given a chance to disarm but did not take advantage of it. In the melee, she critically injured one of our number, and drew blood from another before she was addressed properly."

The Sibulla repeated the answer in a matching neutral tone to the Raja.

"I see." The Raja rubbed his chin, tapping his finger against his lips before turning to his advisor. "Philomene, have her body and weapon brought here. I want to see this woman. Have the reported soil samples and notes brought as well."

"As you command, Great Raja."

As he left the room, the Raja asked, "What were the casualties of our sister and brothers in the faith?"

Philomene heard the answer as he walked out of the throne room and shook his head in disbelief. Of all their swordsmen, mages, and archers, the only casualty the Ulaan had suffered came at the hands of a visiting scholar?

He passed the guards posted at the throne room door at a quick pace, moving down the Hall of Grace towards the royal guardsman on records duty. "Where is the body of the visiting scholar?"

The young man turned and was surprised at being addressed by the advisor to the Raja himself. He stood, recovering quickly. "It is with all the other casualties, Great One."

"Have the scholar's body and all her effects brought to the throne room immediately."

The guardsman moved without question, speaking

to another guardsman posted outside the records room and then returning. The second guard was already heading around the bend when the records guardsman reported back.

"It is being done as we speak, Great One."

"Well done." He patted him on the shoulder and left to return to the throne room.

As he left, he had the burning desire to share what he knew to someone. A scholar, without preparation or forewarning, slaying an Ulaan swordsman and injuring another; it was audacious. Just how many Ulaan did it take to defeat her? The idea was beyond reason. It was the type of tale you told friends and then had to spend hours afterward trying to convince them that you weren't making it up.

He realized then that he had no one to tell. He re-entered the throne room, face neutral, feeling alone.

6

ISLE OF SUTEN

Khiron lay at the foot of the bed of their luxury cabin, his mind a blur of activity. He could still taste the roasted hen from the night before. So succulent and seasoned to perfection, he smiled as he remembered the meal. Its presentation had been so exquisite and artistic that he almost hadn't eaten it. But in the end, hunger prevails over art every time, unless you are the artist. He left only bones behind, stripped clean of every remnant of meat.

He and the Arat had been given first-rate treatment as they sat in their new clothes, fresh from the hot bath treatments and tailors. He couldn't remember the last time he had someone bathe him or cut and comb his hair. He could still smell the tangy fragrance of the oils rubbed into his skin.

As the skies darkened, the Arat had been limited to

the confines of her room, the patrons of the Inn growing more numerous and foolish as the night wore on. It was no place for a young girl to be, and it took good coin for them to agree to let her stay.

He ended that night sleeping in the chair beside the bed after having a massage from a woman with fingers easily stronger than any man he'd known. Muscles that had been tight for years were worked loose, and after the hot bath and oils, he easily felt ten years younger. The next morning they ate, bathed again, donned their new clothes, and booked a large cruiser for their trip.

The Arat told him their destination using the stars for plotting, and he told the captain accordingly. No need to cause confusion or injure an ego by having a child give directions.

Their cabin was spacious, with a massive bed that centered the room. A tall table with a round table-top made of marble stood with two accompanying chairs on the port side of the room. A large wardrobe with a prominent full-length mirror dominated the starboard side of the room, and a desk and chair that looked to be polished mahogany were situated beside the door.

Khiron flipped over the large pack he had on his back and threw it on the bed. "Just how much was in that money pouch you lifted?"

The Arat jumped on the bed by the pack and started jumping up and down, hands and legs outstretched each time she jumped. "Enough. To. Get. Us. There." She yelled out each word between jumps, her face full of excitement.

"What are you doing? Let's see what else is on the ship."

"You go and see," she said, still jumping. "I'm staying right here." He thought he heard a giggle, but she was breathing too hard for him to be sure.

"I think I'll rest here for a few minutes myself." They talked for a short time about something that he didn't remember, and then surprising even himself, he fell fast asleep.

The fragrance of warm cinnamon rolls and hot cider woke him. Sunlight streamed through the round windows that were spaced along the edge of the cabin's ceiling, a warmth that made him feel he was on land, not the sea. It was as if he was yet in a dream. He opened his eyes to see the Arat sitting at a tall round table on the other side of the bed, chewing and grinning at the same time.

"How long was I asleep?"

She giggled. "It's a new day, Khiron. We both slept hard. I can't speak for you, but I have never slept on such a comfortable bed in my life. I didn't know how good it could be." Her tone was merry. "Anyway, we needed the rest."

He rubbed his eyes and ran his fingers through his

hair and was surprised. *That's right, it was cleaned and cut back in Chalice. It's going to take a bit to get used to this.*

"I thought the aroma would wake you. Hurry, before they cool off too much."

There were times of late when he forgot that she was the Arat. There were times when all he saw was an eleven-year-old child, seeing the world through her own eyes and being changed by the normalcy. He liked these times.

He stretched, feeling far fewer aches than usual and literally jumped off the bed. "I would sit and eat that delicious smelling food," he said as he walked passed the table, "but somebody is in my seat." Lunging suddenly, he tickled her. She writhed in uncontrollable laughter, seeking to slip out of his tickling grasp but to no avail. She laughed and laughed until there was the smack of flesh against wood.

"Owww!"

He stopped tickling her and looked her over. "Are you all right?"

"You made me hit my leg on the chair! Can't you see that they're bolted down?"

"I'm sorry. I didn't mean for you to get hurt, I—" She shot out of the chair as he spoke and started jumping on the bed.

"Hah! See if you can catch me this time!" Her smile was as mischievous as it was daring.

He growled. "Trick me will you! Well, you won't fool me twice."

The following minutes were a chaotic rumble of laughing, jumping, running, chasing, kicking and tickling. They both guffawed so hard that they couldn't breathe, laying out on the grand bed like wooden planks, hugging themselves as they sought to inhale through random bursts of chortling. It was many minutes later before they regained control.

Khiron tried to talk, his voice hoarse from the laughter. He got up, holding his stomach, which was as sore as if he had been punched repeatedly. "I guess it's too late for these cinnamon rolls, 'eh?" He picked one up and dropped it back on the tray. The replying chuckle started him up again.

They laughed until he thought he was going to die. She didn't look much better. Who would have thought that laughing would be more taxing than fighting? Too tired to move, he eventually slipped back into sleep.

IT MUST HAVE BEEN the ship's motion that woke him. It also must have been its motion that kept putting him to sleep. The Arat was still sleeping, a slight snore as she lay curled in the fetal position near the edge of the bed.

Tidying up his clothes as quietly as he could, he

slid his sheathed knife into his belt and went up to the deck.

The sailors were taking the cover off a longboat. A man with arms littered with tattoos was inspecting the seams and the hull's integrity. The time and attention to detail he showed was impressive, his finger going over the smooth wood like he was calming a horse.

A voice came from a deck above him. "We're ready whenever you are. These rowers will take you to the shore, but because of the reefs, this is as far as we can go."

He nodded his thanks. "We'll be ready in ten minutes."

"There's no rush. Our chef is preparing you lunch for your journey."

Khiron grinned. "Much appreciated, Captain."

He went back to the cabin and arrived to find the Arat smiling through a yawn, her legs swinging from the end of the bed, her feet a foot higher than the floor. Their traveling pack was secure and ready to go, as was she. "What took you so long?" she asked.

"Lunch. It's being made as we speak."

"Well, let's get topside then. This ship is starting to grow on me." She jumped off the bed and headed to the deck behind him. As she fully emerged, he heard her gasp and turned to see what had happened. She was staring past him, mouth agape. He turned again to see what had caught her attention.

It was stunning. He couldn't fathom how he had missed it just a minute ago. The island inlet was a carpet of white sand that stretched back for what he estimated must be five hundred paces. It stopped at what looked to be a flat-topped mountain range that rose from the island like an outer ring. Two figures, which stood at least eighty feet tall, were carved into the mountain face directly in front of them. Between those two figures was a massive black door that dwarfed the figures that framed it. The door looked to open from its middle, but whether it swung inward or outward, he had no idea. As ancient as it was, he doubted it would open at all. Above the door was etched an enormous lion in mid-leap, and about forty feet above that was the mountain's edge.

Khiron pulled his eyes from the sight and found a sailor. "How large is this island?"

"I don't know. The Captain said it once took him days to make a full circle when he was going to make it a tour destination. That seemed like a long time to me, but it's probably because of the reefs and all. They extend out far in certain areas, and this is one of the few places you can get close."

"Yes," the captain said as he came up from behind them, "if not for the reefs, you could circle it in less than a day at full sail. As far as I have seen, those flat-topped mountains form a circle within the island like an outer ring." He pointed. "That is not the only door in the mountains. A quarter-day journey southeast of this door, there is a temple carved from the mountain with pillars that easily stand fifteen times my height. Saw it while we were riding out a storm a couple years back. Had to anchor off shore and pray to the Ancients we were far enough out. The temple stands much taller than the trees, but there are so few here on the sand that it is a good marker."

The Arat walked up, eyes full of wonder, and something else. "It's beautiful, but are there scary things there?" She winked at Khiron. He struggled to stifle a chuckle.

"Legend holds that there is a vast city beyond that door, but who can say. Not many are willing to come out here anymore since so many ships disappeared in this area over the years. Only specialty ships like mine will bring anyone this close."

A broad-chested sailor came forth carrying a bundle.

"Ah, your lunch has arrived. Place it on the longboat, Jas. Now you two, let us help you onboard."

"Give me a minute," Khiron said and disappeared into the cabin. He emerged quickly and was helped down the ladder and into the vessel. The Arat sat near the bow of the boat, with the rowers sitting at the boat's center on either side. He took a seat on the plank near the bow, making sure that his travel pack was secure.

A quick glance from the rowers to ensure that they

were secure, and they set off.

THE ARAT and Khiron watched the two sailors row steadily to the ship from the sandy shore. "They will be back to collect us tomorrow, Khiron." There was no doubt in her voice as if to reassure him.

"How can you be so certain?"

The incredulity in her expression was almost comical. He turned red as he realized the answer.

She took two handfuls of the white sand in her pudgy hands and watched the longboat depart. "I'm not sure when it will happen," she said, "but I had to be here to witness it."

The questions in his head were legion. He knew that asking just one of them would release the torrent of others he suppressed, so he stayed patient. As they stood within sight of the great door, he figured that he'd have the answers to all of them soon enough.

They walked near the edge of the sand close to the shore and started to make camp east of the great door. They could still see it, and if they stayed low, they wouldn't be easily seen without purposely someone looking for them.

"I wouldn't make camp here, young seer."

Both she and Khiron started, and Khiron unsheathed and extended his sword in one motion.

"Impressive reaction time," the blind Nnesutee said with a smile in his voice. "You are a great benefit to your charge." White sand cascaded down his hooded cloak, the light and motion giving it a sheen.

"Nnesutee? What are you doing here?" The Arat sounded genuinely surprised.

Khiron didn't know how he should feel about it. It was obvious that the man was dangerous and he shouldn't be here. The question of how he had gotten here was only superseded by why?

"I thought I should follow my own advice and see a thing in person." His humorous grin disarmed them as he used his walking staff to move Khiron's sword from his path. "As it is, they already know we are here, but it seems they don't deem us a threat."

"They? How do you know?" Khiron asked. He sheathed his sword.

"Because they are already with us. Let us say no more until afterward." He guided them about seventy steps down the shore and turned inward until they were midway between the mountain face and the sea. With a grace that seemed almost regal, he lowered himself until he laid on his stomach, his staff in the sand behind him about three long paces behind his feet.

Following his example, the Arat laid beside the Nnesutee, her eyes a blend of excitement and fear.

Khiron took off his sword and laid it near the blind

swordsman's, but kept his dagger. As he crawled beside the two, coming along the opposite side of the Arat, he felt a vise-like grip on his arm. The Nnesutee mouthed, "the knife," and pointed back towards the other weapons. Begrudgingly, Khiron pulled the knife from his belt and tossed it a hand's length past the other weapons as a breeze blew a spray of sand over them. He silently wondered if the man was truly blind at all.

They lay in silence as the evening came, watching the first of the twin suns lowering gently below the red, orange and yellow horizon. Waves lapped lightly along the shore as if lulling its children to sleep. The caress of the white crests met longing ivory sands and joined as if one, a seamless unity. Time slipped into eternity as it no longer held any meaning.

Then it struck him, like a cold chill at evening-tide, the sudden realization that the Arat hadn't foreseen the Nnesutee being there. She had been as surprised as he was.

So her sight is limited here, if not completely negated. Was her assurance that the longboat will return for us just an attempt to comfort me? Did she lie?

Replaying her words, she had said the sailors would come to collect them, but she never said that they would be successful. A sense of foreboding descended onto him like a weighted cloak, and he felt something akin to fear.

He flinched at a touch on his hand, the contact

snatching him from his thoughts. The Arat had reached out until she found his hand, and her small grip was now tight around his. He could feel her tension as they waited in expectation, and he tried to emote confidence in the strength of his grip. Warmth filled him, and he knew that even beyond his vow, he would protect her as if she was his child. If this was their end, they would see it together. It calmed him.

Time returned to anonymity, passing with no fanfare—a ripple in a pool ever-expanding, passing in silence, yet ever one with the water. The dying rays of the first sun seemed to draw the light of the second as streaks streamed across the sky.

A sudden thunderclap split the air, and they all flinched as dark descended from the East. A motion drew their heads towards the mountain where, before their unbelieving eyes, one side of the massive black door had swung about thirty degrees outward. A shadow of black covered the darkening blue of night, and from the silence emerged a figure.

Covered in shadow, it strode towards the shore like a beam of night. Regality overwhelmingly marked the figure's bearing. The strides were not the movements of those who mask weakness with the illusion of control. Instead, they reflected the graceful fluidity of the great lions of Karitichus, who ran the plains without fear or equal.

Khiron's stomach was clenched, beads of sweat

forming and falling from his brow like rain from a cloud. Mouth dry and lips suddenly sticky, he would have fled if his legs weren't numb. Threat rolled off the figure in a way that was irrational.

The light of the rising moons met that of the dying suns, revealing a tall man in a dark cloak that hung heavily on wide shoulders. His elbow-length hair flowed freely, white and wavy with what looked to be silver highlights that captured the moonlight in flashes of movement. The sheath of his sword was partially visible on his side, but its hilt was hidden beneath his cloak.

Khiron felt the Arat's grip tighten on his, but he couldn't pull his eyes from the man. He felt that walking before him was a force of will, a being both disciplined and untamed. He finally understood that this was who the Arat needed to see and what a blind man had to experience. He was awed.

As the man reached the shore, he was met by eight dark figures who appeared out of the air itself. A ship sat waiting where the boat had dropped them off, a long ramp descending onto the sand. It was a sleek ship, the color of which Khiron couldn't decipher in the dwindling light.

Where in the name of Dris and every Ancient known and unknown did that boat and those people come from? And how did a ship that size get this close to shore?

Finally coming to himself, he stole a glance at the

Arat. Her eyes were as wide as her mouth was open. Beside her, the Nnesutee's blind eyes looked directly at the man on the shore. His jaw was tight, and his eyes leaked tears that ran down his dusky face in rivulets.

He turned back to see a woman standing beside the man. Her hair looked bone-white in the distance and stood less than a fingertips length from her scalp. The other eight figures were no longer there.

The woman bore no sword, but moonlight reflected off the braces of the sheathed daggers clasped upon her forearms. Whatever she wore, it hugged her skin tightly, revealing a clean-limbed and lithe form. Her movements were sure and graceful as if she moved to music he couldn't hear. Even in the covering dark, he felt his heartbeat's tempo increase. Already racing, he held an irrational fear that he might die on the spot.

The man walked onto the ramp, and the woman followed. She then stopped, turning directly towards them. In a shimmer of moonlight, Khiron saw a beautiful face with almond-shaped eyes that cut through the dark.

He heard the Nnesutee whisper a name as if it was a prayer. "Neftii."

It hung in the air before dissipating, and the woman turned away, disappearing into the ship's dark opening. The ramp lifted from the sand, and impossibly, the ship backed from the shore and quickly faded into the pool of night.

7

THE CALL OF DUST

Zatrin Bei sat in the lotus position; her body suspended an arm's length above the floor in perfect stillness. Her hands rested on her knees, palms up, each cradling a round stone. A light glow radiated from her form, and tendrils of light spread like trip wires to fill the small stone chamber.

Her body secured, her mind searched for the young seer she had seen at the docks of Chalice. The raw power of the young girl had been vast, her potential rivaling the Psionia'Matri, the head of her order. Raw and untrained as she was, the Arat was a bright light to the Sibulla and could be an invaluable resource to the Unified Dimensions. How the young seer had stayed hidden in Zaim for so long was an enigma that no longer mattered. Whatever the cloak of anonymity had been, it was gone. The Arat was in danger.

The dimension blurred before her as she searched for the power signature that she felt when their minds touched. Seas and lands whisked by; blues, whites, greens, and browns streaked together until they became a uniform black, and then in the stillness, she spotted a spark.

Her concentration absolute, the Sibulla focused on that spark. To her perception, it was a lone swirl of silver encased in a tight ball on a sea of nothingness. It grew closer and closer until strands of colors appeared, and a landscape took shape. She had found her.

The Arat sat on white sands with the man she had seen with her in Chalice. And there was another man, whose features were similar to the Master of Swords. *A Nnesutee.* She perceived no other person near them and then saw the door in the massive mountain. There was a mountain wall that ringed as far as she looked, but she could not see beyond its perimeter. Summoning all her strength, she pushed against the indomitable darkness that lay beyond, with no effect. This should not be possible. She abandoned her efforts and shifted back to the Arat, who smiled gingerly as she spoke to the two men. The little girl showed no awareness of her presence.

Suddenly, the Nnesutee looked up, startling her. Zatrin felt his milky white eyes bore into her as if he could see into her very soul. His lip curled as he declared, "Begone!" Eyes snapping open, she was shocked to find herself suddenly back in her chamber.

By the Ancients! This should not be possible!

She slowly descended to the floor, the tendrils dissipating into the ether and the illumination of her shielding now a dwindling vapor. Uncrossing her legs, she rose with deliberation, placing the stones she held in a silver box. She put the box into her trunk, which she then secured.

A knock came at the door. "Arbiter," a muffled voice said, "the Great Raja summons you. I am to escort you to the throne room at your earliest convenience."

She said nothing but stepped before a wall-length mirror to make sure she was presentable. Reaching over to the desk beside the mirror, she picked up her gloves to put them on and saw, to her surprise, that her hands were trembling.

ZATRIN ENTERED the throne room to see that everyone was already in place. At the room's center was a travois where lay the scholar who had been slain by the Ulaan. The scholar was comely, even in Nihil's grasp. Her skin a caramel brown, she looked little more than a young woman deep within the repose of sleep.

Lying on top of her body was a thin short-sword, partially unsheathed. It was single-edged with a square guard and a hilt that was longer than a single-handed grip, but not quite long enough to classify it as a two-handed one. Its craftsmanship marked the sword as being of exceptional quality.

Packages wrapped in papyrus were lined up beside her. A stack of unrolled manuscripts had been placed on a desk that had been brought in and placed about five paces from where she lay. The Raja's advisor, Philomene, was looking them over with a frown. In the distance, she thought she heard the low buzzing of bees.

The Raja spoke from his throne, his tone a fount of respect. "I trust that your accommodations were suitable, Arbiter?"

"Great Raja of Ceidon, Brazen Shield of Mount Ceidon, Ruler of the Kingdom of Zaim; coming from you, they could be nothing less." She moved with a sophisticated air, giving a nod to the Ulaan swordsmen who returned it in like manner. "I take it that placing the sword upon the woman came from you, Master of Swords?" She took her place beside him, noting his focus upon the corpse.

"It did indeed, Arbiter. The honor of every great warrior is to be committed to the next world with their weapon. Her title or station makes no difference."

Philomene lowered the papers he was examining

and took up his post beside the Raja, looking keenly interested in the conversation.

"She was a scholar," UiNemtasma of the Ulaan said dispassionately. "The sword rite is for swordsmen and none other."

The Arbiter gave the Ulaan swordsman a curious glance. "A woman killed one of your swordsman who trained at a dojon dedicated to Dris, injured another such swordsman, and yet is not deemed worthy of the sword rite because of the lack of a title? Titles have their power, but when one demonstrates the definition of a title, have they not attained the right to claim it and all it grants? Tell me, UiNemtasma. Will this issue require an Arbiter to settle it as well?"

Phiomene's brows raised as he looked at the Sibulla with a fresh regard. He then turned towards the Steep Bay as if listening to something beyond.

The Ulaan swordsman bowed, her expression one of concession. "It is right that the Master of Swords have this wish granted before he faces mortal combat. I give no objection."

The Master of Swords remained impassive, his eyes remaining on the body of the deceased.

"Good," the Sibulla said. "As both kingdoms have agreed to the rule of the Dojon of Dris in this matter, only the particulars of what happens after the challenge is settled must be discussed."

A bell rang two times through the chamber; its pitch high and sound sharp.

"Regardless of the outcome," the Arbiter continued, "the people of Mount Ceidon and all of Zaim shall not be harmed, in according with—"

The Raja raised his hand, cutting her off as the bell sounded again. "I acknowledge the Sibulla right of arbitration and the rules of governance that every ruler must follow once the process has commenced, but we have a guest." The Raja pulled one of the rings on his throne's arm, and the doors opened partially, admitting Rephna, the Raja's aide and Royal arm of his will.

She bowed to all present and quickly made her way across the large room to the Raja, stealing a glance at the corpse as she passed by. The Raja leaned close as she spoke into his ear. He nodded and replied so softly that Zatrin could not hear the exchange.

Rephna bowed to him, then once again to all the assembled, and swiftly made her way back out of the room.

"I apologize to you all, and Arbiter, I ask your forbearance." The Raja looked at each of them with solemnity. "A royal from the Isle of Suten has arrived. The people don't know who he is, but for some reason, his arrival at the docks caused quite a stir. Word has spread through the lowlands and reached the Ulaan, who have returned to the Mount, forty-seven in total. It seems that while we have talked, masses of people gathered at the foot of the Mount near the lifts. The royal guards thought that we heard the sound, as it only quieted when the Ulaan arrived."

"The Isle of Suten?" The Raja's brow lined, then his eyes opened with comprehension. "The scholar... She is from the Isle of Suten, not Zuutin."

Zatrin's stomach dropped. The Suten were more legend than real in the minds of most and for almost a half-century had stayed mostly unseen. She could feel the tension thicken in the room.

"I suspend the arbitration and yield the throne room back to you, Great Raja." She bowed, and saw the Raja bow his head thankfully in response. She shot a glance to the corpse, wishing they could have removed the body from the room, but nothing could be done about it now.

How and by the power of what Ancient did the Suten learn of one of their people being killed, and so quickly?

A deep bell rang, and the doors of the throne room opened fully. The royal from the Isle of Suten entered the room. Philomene took an involuntary step backward.

The Suten Royal strode in with an unfeigned authority, a dynamic sense of power filling the air. Bone-white hair with silver streaks hung long, framing a mahogany face, which was darker than the scholar's. Remarkable blue eyes regarded them intently before falling on the corpse of the scholar.

He walked to the fallen Suten with a grace that was almost gentle and removed his cloak, covering the body respectfully. He rose and addressed the Raja. "Great Raja, Shield of Mount Ceidon, and Ruler of Kingdom of Zaim, I am Yaisen'Re Bennu of the Sutenit Tur Antu, the ruling family of the Suten Empire. I am here to collect the body and effects of this citizen of our kingdom and to bring them home."

The Suten wore what could only be called a light armor, though unlike any she had seen. The under-armor seemed to be a type of scaled leather. So dark as to almost look like absence, it hugged close to his skin and covered him from high on his neck to where it disappeared within his boots. His spaulders, vambraces, and rerebraces were made of what looked to be a light, flexible black metal, and followed the form of his muscles beneath, as did his cuisse and greaves of the same material. He stood a head taller than the Nnesutee (who was the tallest of them), with a lithe, chiseled build. His spaulders were shaped in the form of lion heads, and his breastplate followed the form of his body beneath, but it was the thickest of the armor he wore.

The Raja broke his silence with a bow of his head. "You are welcome, Yaisen'Re Bennu of the Suten Empire. As a visiting royal, you are to be granted a throne here and an aide who will address any of your needs or desires."

The Suten shook his head. "That will not be necessary. As a ruler of many, I know well the weight of command and the limitations our roles can place upon us. Instead, I ask for a suspension of the rules of protocol. I see Ulaan, a Sibulla, a Nnesutee, and the bodily remains of one from my kingdom, all sharing your throne room. I request this suspension so that we may speak freely and unhindered by the niceties of expectation."

"In light of the honor you bestow upon us by your presence and your kingdom's loss," the Raja said, "I grant your request." For the first time that she had seen, the Raja gave a genuine smile.

She took note of the Raja's reaction but was struck by what she saw in the Suten himself.

The aesthetic of his color, the structure of his form, his sleek yet rugged handsomeness, and the power that seemed to radiate from him in undulating waves; the man was stunning. Everything about him had the effect of capturing attention. The luminescence of his large penetrating eyes, sheltered under his arched eyebrows, created an effect that drew one's gaze to his face. She had never seen a being so utterly beautiful, or one whose movements seemed so potentially deadly. She felt her heart quicken, and with effort, brought her pulse back under control. Despite his appeal, she was the master of her body and desires, and that she would always be.

The Ulaan watched him silently, and Zatrin took note that they were not pleased.

"You have granted us your name," the Raja said congenially, "and I cannot but reciprocate for all present. This is Philomene, my royal advisor. The Sibulla is Zatrin Bei. She was summoned to our borders to conduct an arbitration between our kingdom and the Ulaan, the cause of which ended the life of one of your most precious citizens. The Ulaan is named, UiNemtasma, and is the ranking member of their delegation. The Nnesutee is our Master of Swords, and as in the tradition of their tribe, they bear no name."

"Iskander, O Sword of Suten. My name is Iskander." In the allure of the presence of the Suten, it seemed that no one had noticed that the Master of Swords had lowered to one knee. Mouths and eyes opened wide at his declaration.

The Suten spoke. "Rise, defender of those in need. You have done well to commit your skills here. I knew the Raja's father; he was a good man, and it seems that trait has passed on to his son. Your service is placed well for this season."

The Raja's eyes opened wider, and a hush fell over the room. "You knew my father? You look not to have seen more than a score of harvests, at the most maybe a few harvests more than that. Nihil claimed the Great Raja of Rajas two score harvests ago."

The Suten nodded knowingly. "Jk'bar has many benefits. I knew him. His infectious laughter, his predilection for red wine, his endless patience, and his love for the people of Zaim. Few could match his skill with the bow, but he would never let my father send a healer for his elbow."

The Raja's breathing quickened, his eyes watery but not spilling over.

"Jk'bar," the Ulaan spokeswoman said in disbelief. "That is a discipline only possible for the most skilled of masters. Surely you dissemble!"

The Suten ignored her, continuing to address the Raja. "Your kingdom has never been in threat from the Suten, and will continue to be safe from us as long as just men and women hold the seat of Raja."

He turned to the Nnesutee. "Iskander, am I right to believe that you were to defend the honor of Zaim by right of combat according to the rules of Dris?"

"As ever, Sword of Suten."

"And it was an Ulaan that stole our scholar's life?"

"No truth escapes your sight, Suten Lord."

Zatrin Bei's head swooned as she watched what was transpiring. She felt unbalanced. In the time it took a flash rain to evaporate beneath the twin sun's gaze, this Suten Lord had taken control the Kingdom of Zaim. What was his intent? What should her response be? She knew that she looked solid to the naked eye, but she felt frayed below the surface. The rebuke that the Nnesutee accompanying the Arat had given her should not have been possible. Her sight being blocked from the Suten Isle should not have been possible. And now, a Lord from that very Isle had captured a kingdom with the power of his presence and words alone. It was incomprehensible.

Since the Second Age, the Sibulla had been the arbiters of kingdoms, and the living history of all her forebears and contemporaries was in her active memory, Yet, her experiences today were new. Her world had changed, and in that refashioning she knew that the rest of her sect had changed too.

The Suten Lord walked to the body lying under his cloak, the pathos in his expression was plain. "Great Raja, it is our belief that every Suten be interred in Suten soil. It is a tradition we have held religiously for over an Age, and it is one of the reasons I have come. We are the land, and the land calls for its own. I ask your leave to return the body of our scholar and all her effects to our Isle. I seek to do this immediately."

"It is our grace to honor your custom as we would ask you to accept ours if positions reversed. As you have asked, it is granted."

"No," UiNemtasma said.

Everyone in the room turned to the Ulaan. The Suten Lord looked up, his gaze deep and unreadable.

"We are in an arbitration," UiNemtasma said, "and the rulership of Zaim is currently in dispute. The body stays here until the challenge is completed and the arbitration is settled. If, and only if, the Nnesutee is successful in defeating me can the Suten Royal have his...corpse." A hint of disgust marked her last word.

She had declared this to the Sibulla, and not to the Raja or the Suten Lord, following the rules of arbitration as if they hadn't been lifted.

"You are foolish, Ulaan," the Suten Lord said, rising to his full height. "It is clear your thinking is limited and that you need assistance in this matter. I will illuminate you. I am not defined by any rules of Dris, nor am I limited from eradicating you and your kingdom from existence."

An open threat! Zatrin Bei found that she was holding her breath. *By tradition and protocols that can't be dismissed by a ruler, the Suten Lord has ensured that the arbitration will not resume until this new threat has been addressed. In the same breath, he has forced me to be a witness to this new issue, and possibly to have to stand as an arbitrator for it if he so requests. Me'ett's mercy, he is too brilliant by far. Brilliant, and yet foolish to challenge the Ulaan. Who is this man?*

The Suten spoke to the Ulaan like she was a toddler. "You speak for your kingdom as if you were one of the Nine. You aren't. You are completely ignorant of where you stand and who you stand before." His eyes fell upon UiNemtasma. "You are a swordsman, nothing more. You have no power here. All your leverage evaporated when the Great Raja suspended the rules."

UiNemtasma started to speak and then stopped herself. Her dual-hued face darkened as she comprehended the truth of his words. She had been outwitted and dishonored, and she had no argument to counter it. Rage filled her eyes.

The Suten Lord lifted his cloak from the scholar, then looked at the table where her papers lay. "We have the Raja's permission. Collect her things and transport her to the ship."

It looked for a moment that the Suten Lord had detached from reality, speaking to himself, then figures appeared out of nowhere wearing light armor over dark fabric. Black masks that resembled the metal of the Suten Lord's armor covered their faces.

Everyone jumped and Philomene gasped in surprise as two such figures materialized near him as they approached the table.

"Impossible," UiNemtasma exclaimed.

"Why?" The Suten Lord's tone was pedantic. "Because the process your Ancient used and which made your skin its dual hue, is supposed to block magery? Oh, was that supposed to be a secret?" His grin was feral.

UiNemtasma's body shook in barely held restraint as the body of the scholar was lifted. The doors opened, and the body was carried out by the only two figures who remained visible.

As they left, a woman with short bone-white hair and adorned in the same leather-like armor as the Suten Lord, appeared next to him, handing him a scabbarded sword. It was thin with an ornately crafted hilt, a large blue gem embedded in its pommel. She spoke to him in a language Zatrin didn't recognize and then stood by his side.

Zatrin watched them carefully. The woman was stunningly beautiful, but in a different way than her lord. Her hue was similar to the Suten Lord's, but her eyes resembled those of the Master of Swords: almond-shaped, and lined with kohl. She didn't carry a sword but had a long dagger sheathed on each forearm. Her lean muscles flexed through her armor with every move.

Something is wrong here. They are not leaving. The Suten Lord is waiting for something— She came to a decision.

"Great Raja." She spoke with as much control as she could muster. "As the arbitration is suspended indefinitely, my role is temporarily unneeded. I request leave to retire to my chamber."

The Raja looked with understanding and nodded his assent. "As you wish, Arbiter. I will send for you when it is time for the arbitration to recommence."

She approached the doors with a measured gait and stepped into the hall.

"Stop!" The voice came from before her and not behind. Approaching from the opposite end of the grand hall were three Ulaan. The lead Ulaan wore a white cowl with no cloak and seemed to glide across the floor towards her.

One of the Nine! She turned from the approaching Ulaan to see the Suten Lord standing without expression, his hand resting on the pommel of his sword.

She was too late.

8

CASTING STONES

They sat in silence, the longboat quickly pulling further from the shores of the Island. The cascading water from the oars made the only sound as the experienced sailors were not slapping the water as they rowed. Khiron sat at the bow, looking back upon the Arat.

She hadn't spoken much since the previous evening. She looked thoughtful, and Khiron wondered if somehow seeing the Suten had changed her. She had entered the craft first and sat near the stern, and now she stared out towards the great door in the mountain.

With reticence, they had walked up to the imposing sight at first light. The Nnesutee had assured them that they were alone, but the feeling of being watched never fully lifted. Scenes of nature at balance stood in relief across the span of the door, the craftsmanship beyond telling. The Arat touched the images, running her hand over the shapes as she walked. Khiron also touched the dark metal and was surprised to find it warm.

The Nnesutee had walked to the shore while they lingered near the door. He had sat wrapped in his cloaks, his face hidden in the depths of its cowls, facing the supple waves, just as he was doing now on the longboat. With his walking staff lay across his lap and his arms nestled within the folds of his sleeves, the blind man sat facing towards the West. Khiron wondered how long he would stay with them, or if he would stay at all. Surprisingly, he had begun to feel comfortable with the man around.

No questions were asked when the sailors saw the Nnesutee with them. They helped the ageless man onto the longboat and set out for the ship without a word.

The journey was quick. The Captain greeted them with warm tea and cider as they came aboard, the twin suns standing at their apex. "I am glad you all are well." He glanced at the Nnesutee, who was being assisted onto the deck. "We have alternate quarters for a single occupant. I will have it prepared immediately."

"That won't be necessary," the Nnesutee said as he approached. "A dry place on deck will be fine."

"Nonsense, we would never allow such a thing on

the Sea Blade. It would sully my reputation." The Captain motioned to one of the sailors with a quick flip of his head. "Prepare the meditation cabin for our new guest."

The Nnesutee bowed deeply. "Thank you, Captain. My eyes can't use the sunlight anymore, but I can still feel its caress. The moonlight has a different feel, but both are packed with memories that comfort my soul. While you tidy the cabin, please allow space for me on the deck as well. Other than a good bath, I would consider this deck a treasure."

The Captain rested a hand on his shoulder. "I'll be happy to do so. One of my crew will guide you to it after we get underway. Now, we've prepared hot baths for your friends while on our way to the Island and have more than enough water to accommodate you."

"Thank you, Captain. Coin, I have in little supply, but I have other gifts. May I feel your face?"

The Captain hesitated. His mouth opened as if to speak, but he said nothing. He closed it, and then took the Nnesutee's hands and brought them to his face.

The Nnesutee felt his face, his hair, and even his neck. He lifted his hands from his skin and smiled. "Thank you, Captain. Some coal from the fire and some of the thick paper you use for your supply lists would do nicely after a bath. I prefer to work in the open air."

"It will be done. The bath cabin is this way."

Placing the Nnesutee's hand upon his shoulder, the Captain led him to the cabin himself.

Khiron entered their cabin to see the Arat sitting on the grand bed, her legs crossed. Two of the round stones she played with on numerous occasions sat in her upturned hands. Her face was a mask of concentration. Suddenly her hands fell, eyes opening with a frown, and she sighed.

"You going to stand there and watch me all day or are you going to get us something to eat?"

He grinned at her. "I don't know. Depends on what the chef is cooking."

"For what we paid, it better be whatever we want." She put the stones back into her stone pouch and tightened the end sack. "I have to say, though, I'm surprised by the amount of money that was in this pouch. In every vision, I saw myself taking it from him, but I can't shake the feeling he brought it for me all along. Almost as if he was aware."

"It's plausible," he shrugged, "but you would know better than me." Lifting the strap of the traveling sack over his head, he laid it on the desk near the door. "What happened back there on the island? It seemed different for me than it was for you." Sitting down on the edge of the bed, he lowered his voice. "You said the

Island was a place you felt that you had to go. Why was it so important? Did you see what you expected?"

She looked at him in thought, and then her eyes grew wide, and she smiled. She snatched up her stones from the bed. Taking a long breath, she settled herself, controlling her excitement.

"Casting stones are known for being talismans that give glimpses of the future," she said. "They aren't. Those who use them as such are charlatans or people with little of the gift who need the pageantry of myth to cover the times when they see nothing." She lifted one into the light. "In truth, they are foci. They help us center ourselves and serve as an anchor to the present."

"Like people who walk in their sleep and tie themselves to a post with a short lead to make sure they don't go far?"

She giggled. "Something like that. A better description would be from last night when I held your hand. I was able to witness everything before me because I knew you were there with me. The assurance of your presence allowed me to not have to look away. It grounded me, making things clear by relating the potential present and future to this true timeline." She lowered the stone and put both of them back into the bag, sealing it.

"Was what you saw what you expected to see?"

"That's just it. I didn't have any expectations. It is one of the few places where I had no sight."

He rubbed his head, looking confused.

"I had to know if it was something wrong with me or if it was something to do with the place itself. Not being able to see much about the Nnesutee on the ship the other day gave me a hint. Still, like he said, I needed to see with my eyes so I could understand what I could not see with my gift."

A brow raised. "Then how did you know you weren't in danger when the Atiere hunters threatened you if you couldn't see them with your gift?"

She covered her mouth with a false look of shock. "Oh my, what was I thinking? Guess it's a good thing I had no problem seeing the future currents of the Atiere, 'eh? Or my own for that matter." Her mischievous giggle filled the cabin.

He chuckled. "No, you don't. We're not going through that again." Then he chuckled some more.

Her smile fell. "I needed to go to the island because at the center of every stream of possible futures I see, is a negation, a blind spot."

"The island," he said with certainty.

"The island," she said with a nod. "My future, our future, all futures, rest on the fate of that Island. I needed to see it to understand, and I was certain that if I didn't make it to the Island by yesterday, I would miss my chance forever. It was a risk, but I was determined to make it, no matter the cost."

He released a long exhale and sat back. From stealing the royal advisor's purse to her dogged determination to get to the island by yesterday, what pressure it must have been on her. His expression was warm when he looked at her again.

"You know that what you did was incredibly dangerous. If not for the Nnesutee's help along the way, neither of us would probably be here. Was it worth it?"

Her sad grin shook him. "What is life without purpose? Gifts can be both burden and blessing, but knowing a gift's purpose is what makes one appreciate it. A thing of intrinsic value can be discarded or cursed by a person without knowledge of its worth, and often is. My gift of sight has shown me much more than a person should have to deal with. Some of the potential streams of my own future are stronger than others, and some of those aren't pleasant. I've struggled because I've had no purpose guiding me; no understanding. Even with strong streams, the future is not certain. As the present races forward, streams grow, change, even disappear; but having purpose locks a point in the raging current. It creates a focus, an anchor of stability that adds stability to all the streams." She reached out and touched his cheek, eyes filled with tears. "Khiron, I finally know my purpose. I have found the strength to face the future. I was lost amidst the streams, but now I know where I am. I was blinded by the currents, but now I can see."

Khiron tried to speak and found he couldn't. He felt drips on his hands and realized that he was crying. She wiped his eyes and then hugged him tight, dampening his shirt with her own. He hugged her back. They were family. Neither let go.

KHIRON FOUND the Nnesutee sitting on the deck topless, twisting his hair into braids while it was still wet. His left arm was a sleeve of tattoos of symbols he didn't understand but looked purposeful in their design. Seeing him in the light after his bath, the man seemed to be much younger than he first thought.

"How was the bath?"

The Nnesutee grinned wide, his ivory teeth glistening. "I had forgotten how good they can feel. Washed my clothes too. Now that took some time. You know when clothes are clean by the smell and the feel. The Captain offered to have it done, but I don't like people I don't know handling my things."

"I understand the sentiment."

"How is our young seer?"

"Sleeping. She ate her meal and then went fast asleep."

"It was a long night and morning," the Nnesutee said. He started working on a new braid.

"Shouldn't you comb it out and wait until it dries?"

He flashed another grin. "With my lifestyle and the locales I end up in, trust me, this way is the best way for my needs."

The suns had begun to sink beneath a floor of glassy gray, birds chirping as they flew towards the coastal trees of Baciliesa, which grew dark in the distance. They sat for another hour in relative silence until the moons had unmoored themselves from the bounds of Gaia and lifted into the evening sky.

The Nnesutee donned his shirt and pulled one of his cloaks around his shoulders. His breath was visible in the cooling air; his voice barely discernible above the waves when he spoke. "She is going to be okay, even better in the morning."

Khiron turned towards him, then back to the moonlight, reflecting like a path across the Silver Sea.

"What she did yesterday, what she witnessed was necessary."

"I know," Khiron said. "She is different now. A good different, but I will miss the little girl in her. Increasingly, she sounds more like an aged woman than a child. How her words and mannerisms shift so suddenly disturbs me at times."

"Both of you have changed, but she is still only eleven. She can be that part of herself with you freely, and that is a gift she needs more than she knows. You love her like a father, and she will need that love in the days ahead, for she is in more danger now than ever before."

"What do you see about this danger specifically?"

The Nnesutee turned and looked at him with his eyes open, milky white corneas with light grey irises that seemed to look through him, leaving nothing hidden. "Nothing you haven't ascertained on your own." He closed his eyes, turning back to the sea. "What you witnessed on the island," he paused, "very few people get to see and live. Did you notice your cloak and shirt?"

"What do you mean?"

"Feel the back of your shirt behind where your heart is."

Khiron reached behind his back and reached up, feeling two cuts in the fabric. He frowned, not understanding.

"Neftii."

He remembered the woman who stood by the man on the shore, the long regard she had given them, Nnesutee's saying her name and his tears. He started, realizing how the cuts had been made. "When?"

"Just before you threw your knife back by the swords."

Despite the cold, he was sweating. "Dris' beard! It seems I owe you a debt."

"It was not my presence that spared you. I believe she saw purpose in the girl and spared her, and in you too."

The ship groaned softly as it turned around the southern end of the continent in a northerly direction. Khiron stood gingerly, his unanswered questions about the woman and how the Nnesutee knew her were no longer important to him. This day had been a heavy one for him, yet through the weight, he felt a sense of peace.

"We've booked passage all the way to the shores of Karitichus. We'll make stops every few days or so to restock and spread our legs a bit. You are welcome to come with us as long as you'd like."

The Nnesutee nodded.

"I've heard that your tribe doesn't use proper names, but it's strange traveling with you and not knowing how to address you. For the Arat's sake, what would you like to be called?"

It was barely louder than an exhale, but the words were clear in the night air. "Ally."

9

———

ULAAN

The three Ulaan crossed the threshold of the throne room in a triangle formation. Each wore leather armor which was reinforced around vital areas, the metal buckles and studded vambraces dulled to give no shine. Their swords were worn in the tradition of Dris — one sheathed on the back, and one on the side — and a dark substance had been painted across their eyes in a line, crossing the bridge of their noses as if linking the vertically split halves of blue and gold hues together.

They stopped when they saw the two Suten standing near the room's center. At a motion from the woman standing point, the swordsmen behind her flowed out, flanking her on both sides. Of the three, she alone wore a cowl with no cloak. Establishing position, she pulled it back.

"I am Ueeha, of the Nine of the Ulaan, and by the Rule of the Sword of Dris, this kingdom should already be ours." She paused as she looked at the two Ulaan representatives, who stood with their gazes averted, eyes cast downward. "It is my understanding that before we could finalize our expansion here and declare victory, a Sibulla intervened." She turned to Zatrin Bei. "I state formally that the Nine had no knowledge of your presence in this kingdom. If we had, we would have chosen to give this land the benefit of living under our banner at a later time. We meant no disrespect to your Order, nor to your person."

Zatrin Bei gave a fractional nod, her eyes never leaving the Ulaan leader. "It is and will be so noted."

Ueeha's gaze shifted to the Great Raja, controlled anger in her eyes. "I also understand that upon knowledge of the Sibulla's presence and request, arbitration commenced in compliance with the Qio'Nadri, the Sibulla compact that, I trust, we all follow. During said arbitration, the challenge of Dris was invoked, issued, and accepted under the witness of the Sibulla herself, leaving the leadership of this land to the fate of the sword in single combat." Her expression softened, the hint of a grin at the corner of her lips. "Is this so?"

Silence fell upon the throne room like a leaf falling from a tree. It lingered before being broken by the Raja's voice, his face a block of granite.

"Welcome Ueeha, of the Nine." His voice was

devoid of emotion. "Most is as you have said. I commend you for the quality of your intelligence."

"Most?"

The Raja licked his lips, his nose flaring momentarily as if in indignation. "The Kingdom of Zaim is sovereign and has been led by my forebears for eight generations. Your suggestion that my kingdom should be a vassal to yours is a statement of conjecture, is not accepted, nor will I substantiate it by tacit agreement." He sat back and took in the Ulaan leader with a gelid stare.

"Thank you, Great Raja of Ceidon, Brazen Shield of Ceidon, Ruler of all Zaim." The edge of her lips curved upward ever so slightly as she spoke. "I am glad to have agreement between our two kingdoms. Suggestion and conjecture should always be put aside for the truth that is revealed by the sword. As the Ancient whom we both worship teaches, truth is revealed in combat." Her eyes hardened as she turned to UiNemtasma. "Who issued the right of challenge?"

"It was the Nnesutee, Great One; the Raja of Ceidon's Master of Swords."

Ueeha's glance took in the Nnesutee, who stood alone about twenty paces from the Raja's throne, and then went back to UiNemtasma. "Why does he yet live? This arbitration is a simple one. Why is there delay? By Dris, our honored Sibulla was leaving the chamber when I arrived." Her tone became baleful. "Why is this arbitration not over?"

Zatrin Bei could feel the tension in the room. Before her stood arguably one of the most dangerous swordsmen in all the kingdoms of Gaia. The Ulaan respected power, and as a Sibulla she represented that beyond measure, but she felt anything but.

She flinched. There was a sudden presence on the edge of her mind. *What? Ah... The Psionia'Matri seeks to witness this through my eyes.* She opened herself to the leader of her Order, allowing her to see and hear through her eyes and ears, but keeping access to her thoughts secure. As she spoke, the presence of her leader added weight to her words, the power of her station and role riding every syllable. "There are customs to be observed and processes that take time, Ueeha of the Nine of the Ulaan. I recognize your presence here and grant your right as a ruler to speak for your kingdom. The terms granted to UiNemtasma are held, but her right to speak for the Ulaan is hereby revoked."

The Ulaan Leader nodded her agreement. "As you have said, so shall it be."

Zatrin felt, rather than heard, Philomene's sudden exhalation, but it didn't feel to her that the tension in the room had abated. There was something not quite right. Like torchlight suddenly flooding a darkened room, it became clear to her. For the entire time Ueeha had been in the room, she had avoided looking at the Suten.

Yaisen'Re had remained poised near the room's center with the almond-shaped eyed Suten standing beside him. He had watched the proceedings with what appeared to be an air of utter indifference. Something was going on here between the Suten and the Ulaan that had yet to be revealed. She opened her thoughts so that the Psionia'Matri could become aware of her realization, then closed them again. A sense of curiosity and expectation filled her.

"Great One," UiNemtasma said with great deference, "Zaim would be ours, but the arbitration was suspended by the Raja upon the arrival of—"

"I ended it." The voice rang clear, commanding.

Everyone turned to the Suten royal, his stare now boring into the Ulaan leader. For the first time, her eyes met his.

"Your kingdom seeks to be an Empire?" His grin was feral. "You have grown arrogant in your isolation."

Ueeha stiffened, her lips a tight line.

The Suten stepped closer to her. The force of his presence, which somehow he had held in check since Ueeha and her two guards had come, now flooded the throne room. "You Ulaan know who we are, and yet you would kill a citizen of my Empire? You are not ignorant of our conquests, yet you would deem it a small thing to draw our attention?"

UiNemtasma stepped forward enraged. "You speak to one of the Nine! Empire? You have an Island!" She moved her hand to her sword's hilt when Ueehaa raised her hand sharply. UiNemtasma stepped back in shock as if physically slapped by the force of the order.

The Suten Lord's eyes broadened in sudden awareness and then looked almost amused. "You haven't taught them. The rulers of the great Ulaan people, feared by every kingdom for their martial skill, have not taught their people about the Suten Empire? Pathetic. To remove a catechism of Dris from a dojon that follows him is," disgust filled his tone, "abominable. When a religion loses its faith—" He let his sentence drop unfinished.

Zatrin Bei watched Philomene the Guileless' brow furl, its lines deep, and then his sudden look of comprehension. "No!" he cried out uncharacteristically. "It can't be possible!" He grasped the arm of the Raja's throne, the flesh of his fingers becoming white as he squeezed.

Ueeha was livid, her anger barely controlled. The two Ulaan who flanked her stood still as statues, but uncertainty marked their gazes.

Shifting his stance, Yaisen'Re handed his sword to his fellow Suten. She received the sword, bowed her head, and stepped back.

"I am Yaisen'Re Bennu of the Sutenit Tur Antu, the royal family of the Suten Empire, and I challenge you,

Ulaan. I know the conquest that you intend, but you are not worthy of conquering Gaia. None unworthy should conquer this dimension, and while we are here, none shall." He shifted his head, his hair falling over his face, his bright eyes partially shadowed by his unbound mane which resembled a great cat hunting in tall grass. "It seems that this day has been long in coming. So be it, the wait is over. I am here."

Everyone stood in shock, all the Ulaan swordsmen taking a step backward as if pushed. There was power released in the Suten's pronouncement, and it was if the land itself recognized it.

Zatrin suddenly felt unmoored. The Sibulla were feared and respected across the dimensions, yet all her abilities and the weight of the history of her order, seem to mean nothing at this moment. What was happening here was having an effect beyond the dimension. She felt through their connection that even the Psiona'Matri seemed to lose her centering. She let her consciousness expand passed the physical plane and felt ripples moving in the cosmic before being repelled back into herself. All her senses dimmed sharply, then slowly began to recover, her training the only thing keeping her standing. She checked for the leader of her Order's presence. It was still with her, but greatly diminished.

"To remove a catechism from a dojon is a violation of the code of all swordsmen," the Suten Lord said, "whether they are in a dojon of Dris, or not. It is also an unquestionable sign of cowardice and an abdication of honor." He turned to Zatrin Bei. "I officially remove my suspension of the arbitration. That balance may be judged proper in the Ancient's Me'ett's eyes and the compact upheld with the Sibulla as a whole, the Master of Swords shall have his duel with UiNemtasma. I will face the Ulaan in the evening, following the conclusion of that arbitration. Neftii," he motioned to the white-haired Suten standing near him, "will be my second." Without pause, he turned to the Raja. "I deem this acceptable to you?"

Stunned, the Raja of Ceidon nodded his agreement. It was only when Philomene touched him that he realized he wasn't speaking. He cleared his throat. "I agree to the declaration of the Suten Lord, reinstate all protocols, and yield the arbitration to the Sibulla, Zatrin Bei."

The Suten's heavy stare fell on the Sibulla, boring through her like sunlight through gossamer. She understood the possible ramifications of witnessing that which was to come and felt the weight of worlds. Gathering her strength, she spoke. "I accept the role of witness in this arbitration between the kingdom of the Ulaan and the kingdom of Zaim, and declare by the power of my office that the outcome of this honor match falls under the rule of Dris and therefore will be binding. It will commence tomorrow morning, an hour past sunrise, at Swordsman's Fate."

The Ulaan Leader began to object, but Zatrin silenced her. "The challenge has already been given and accepted concerning your kingdom and the kingdom of Zaim. You may decline the challenge of the Suten, but that is not now under my jurisdiction. I will see all at Swordsman's Fate in the morn." With that she nodded to the Raja and turned as if to leave.

"Great Raja of Ceidon," the Suten Lord said with great solemnity. "Sovereign Lord of this great city and all its citizens, please allow as many of those who amass at the base of the mount to be brought up. It is my belief and wish that the battle between your Master of Swords and the Ulaan be witnessed and shared by all. I would consider it a personal favor." With that, the Suten left the chamber.

Silence rushed in like a living thing, the room suddenly marked with a sense of emptiness. Ueeha stood motionless, her expression unreadable. It seemed like an eternity before she pulled up her cowl and left the room, her coterie following in her wake.

10

A DUEL OF FAITH

Heart-shaped leaves leaned listlessly westward before coming to rest, their reddish and yellowing tint a splash of color before a blue and vanilla sky. A lone hawk circled high above the mesa, its wide arcs unhurried as if curious about the busy scene below.

The Master of Swords stood on the edge of Swordsman's Fate speaking with the Suten woman, Neftii. The dueling stage was a circle of stone approximately thirty paces in diameter that stood a hand's span above the ground. The Ulaan sat in a single row around its perimeter, fifty-one in number. Behind them was an open space where the royal guardsmen of Mount Ceidon stood at attention, the tips of their long spears glinting a foot above their helms. Throngs sat behind them, a sea of people filling the area reaching as far back as the palace gates.

Zatrin Bei stood composed but concerned. She was fully recovered from the events of the previous day, but the impending battle between the Suten royal and the Ulaan leader seemed to augur a shift in the streams of the future. There was a structure to the events coalescing around her, but recognition of what it was eluded her. Nevertheless, she suspected that an Ancient's will was being contested, and that could bode ill for many.

The report had come that the Suten ship had set sail an hour prior. Why it had left without the Suten Lord and his second had been a short-lived topic of discussion. What it meant for the Suten Lord's future plans was a matter for consideration, but it would have to wait until after the duels. Depending on the outcomes, there may not be anything to consider.

As she looked out upon the crowds, full smiles and rapid talk were evident everywhere; the excitement probably as much for being on the Mount as much as to witness the duel. Wide eyes attempted to soak everything in: the architecture, the landscape, colors. The lowlanders were in a new universe. She could only imagine the glee they felt at finally seeing what the majority of them had dreamed about for a lifetime.

The Mount of Ceidon was a city within a city that could only be accessed by the lifts and moveable platforms upon its side. Only those who worked the lifts and those who bore the Badge of Ceidon were traditionally allowed up. Of the three hundred or so families that lived upon the Mount, she doubted more than a score of them had descended to the lowlands other than to travel abroad. It was a two-tiered social system, and thus far, it had been successful. Today marked history for Zaim, for never had there been so many people from the lowland on the Mount.

She looked through the gathered Ulaan and frowned. Ueeha of the Nine was not amidst their number. Was she not accepting the Suten's challenge? She scanned the crowds looking for any sign of her until she saw the Raja approaching. As he came close, he smiled at her, bringing her focus squarely on her role as chief witness. He looked refreshed.

There was a hush as the Raja of Ceidon stepped onto Swordsman's Fate to address the gathered crowd. He opened his arms wide.

"My beloved people of Zaim," he said. "Today, we herald back to the traditions of our ancestors and walk out the tenets of our faith. The Ancient Dris teaches us that justice is not found in the sword, but in the heart that wields it. He teaches that skill honed of discipline matters, but when faced with another bearing such skill, the just heart prevails. As it was in the days of old, so it is now.

"Our Master of Swords is not born on our shores

but has pledged his life to defend our kingdom. He has pledged his life in the service of you." He let the word linger, turning full circle to look at all the crowd.

Zatrin felt a shift in the crowd, an expectancy growing within them.

"The Ulaan are known far and wide, and their swordsmanship is said to have no equal, and yet, a just heart cannot be discounted. The result of this match will not change the majority of your lives, but it could change the character of our kingdom. We are valued for our rich crops, which feed people across much of Gaia, but that is not what makes us special. We are challenged for the strength of our yields, but that is not where lies our strength. We are envied for the sweetness of our apples, the heartiness of our corn, the suppleness of our leather, the richness of our olives. Yet, that is not where our strength is found."

Despite the futility of the effort, a feeling of exhilaration washed through her as she watched the Raja speak. She felt the crowd unifying, differences between the highborn and the low falling away. They sat erect across the length of the span, faces focused as they listened. A sense of pride had been sparked within them, and she felt it growing like a brush-fire.

"Does our strength lie in how we feed the soil, or in the tireless care we take in pruning and supporting young plants? Does it lie in how we purify our water and make sure that both human and beast are fed?

Does it lie in the quality nets of our fishing boats, or our ports being kept clean and repaired? Does it?" He paused, cupping the back of his ear as if listening for an answer.

"Noooo!" the crowd roared.

"That's right, my beloved. No! Our value is not in our crops or fields, or yields, or livestock. Our value lies in our people. Our value lies in us. Our love for the land and for all that lives on it. Us."

"Us!" the crowd shouted in unison.

"Us!" He stepped forward, opening his arms even wider.

"Our values are in our families, our friends, our loved ones; our ideas and ideals; our hopes and our dreams; our sweat and our tears, our babies and our dead, our strengths and our weaknesses. Our values are in us! We are the land! We are its waters! We are the soil! We are the kingdom!"

A roar erupted from the Mount, its sound so great it seemed as if the land itself cried out. Its pitch and volume were such that she knew it could be heard for leagues in every direction. People stood and raised their arms to the heavens, euphoric as they were swept in a torrent of pride. She felt the euphoria, her nape hairs tingling in the excitement, but her face remained a neutral mask.

The Raja stood tall, letting himself be caught in the current for a moment before coming back to what needed to be done. He motioned for everyone to sit, and slowly people began to lower themselves back to the ground, the cry of exultation lingering in the air, the atmosphere charged.

He waited until all were seated and then, with a regal gait, walked back to the center of the circle. He spoke calmly and softly enough that the people would have to be silent to hear him, yet his voice carried. "As Raja, I serve the kingdom of Zaim. The Sword of our Kingdom," he motioned to the Master of Swords, "serves the same. We both serve you. We both are you.

"Today, he will engage in combat with an Ulaan, known across the kingdoms for their tremendous skill. She is a woman who has discipline, and who worships Dris as we do. The difference between her and our master of swords is simple; she doesn't serve you.

"She yields the sword like you tend the soil, but there is no love in her yielding. She worships Dris as you worship Dris, but there is no justice in her heart. She reads the teachings we read, yet she arrives at different understandings."

He pointed to the Nnesutee. "This is the difference between them. He is you. He is all of us. Witness the difference between skill fueled by justice and just skill alone. Witness the holy scriptures of Dris interpreted correctly before your very eyes! We are Zaim, and we are just; as it is written, the just heart shall prevail! We are Zaim!"

The crowd leaped to its feet shouting, "Zaim! Zaim! Zaim!" The refrain rose as if from nowhere, growing faster and faster until the sound exploded into a deafening roar.

His face serious, the Raja lifted his hands and motioned to the crowd to settle down. It took some time, but slowly the shouts of pride lowered back to the low rumble of excited discussion. He walked to the Master of Swords, spoke into his ear, then made his way to the short tower that looked over Swordsman's Fate.

The circular, three-level building, was where the royals and their guests had watched duels since the founding of the kingdom. Three thrones faced outwards towards the dueling circle, and in one of them sat the Suten Lord, face partially hidden in a deep cowled cloak. The Raja entered and swiftly sat on the center throne. He leaned to his left, and she read his lips, "I was taught all that by my father."

The Suten's cowl turned, his cerulean eyes exuding an unexpected warmth. "Then you understand why I had to be here."

The Raja straightened, looking out at his people. There was peace in his features, and ever so subtly, he relaxed.

Zatrin Bei watched it all from the side of Swordsman's Fate. Despite the proceedings, she felt a sense of relief for the Raja. She had discerned his inner struggles when she arrived and could feel that the Suten had lifted them immensely. He could handle the weight now. The speech he just gave said as much. She knew that without the Suten, he could have never given one like that. If the Master of Swords succeeded, Zaim would have a stronger ruler than it did just a day prior.

She looked at the Master of Swords, and he nodded, then to UiNemtasma, who did the same. The Ulaan ranks hadn't moved when the Raja spoke, but she could feel the unspoken confidence in them. Despite the Raja's words, they expected their fellow Ulaan to make short work of this duel. She swallowed hard, fighting back emotion, for she felt the same. She walked to the center of the circle.

"Master of Swords come forth." The Nnesutee came forth, wearing his familiar silver robe with the fruit vine standard of Zaim embroidered on its back. He carried a naked thin-bladed, single-edged sword in his left hand, the hilt wrapped in a crossed silver design. Taking his position, he stood calmly.

"Ulaan swordsman, come forth." The Ulaan was clothed in her leather armor and flowed across the circle with light feet. She kept both her swords sheathed and took a position across from the Master of Swords.

Zatrin raised her arms. "According to the tradition of Dris, this challenge ends with death. Its decision is irrevocable. The match begins when the Raja tolls the bell. May the deserving kingdom find favor in their Ancient's eyes."

She backed off of the dueling circle and lowered her arms, giving the nod to the tower. A bell sounded, and the match began.

PHILOMENE THE GUILELESS STOOD SHOCKED. The Ulaan's quickness was inhuman, her attacks so swift that they were difficult to follow. Everything he had ever heard about the Ulaan he saw first hand. In quickness, skill, and agility, he had never seen the Ulaan's match.

When the bell rang, marking the beginning of the duel, Philomene thought that it was already over. The Ulaan's attack had been a blur of leather and steel, and he was surprised that, somehow, the Master of Swords had rebuffed it. Now fifteen breaths into the duel, the Ulaan attacked in bursts, both swords a mixture of thrusts and swings. It was a wonder to behold.

The two seemed to float more than stand, their movement like a dance upon water. Her attacks were the strikes of a viper, his movements a dandelion seed in the wind. She was a cheetah's burst, and he a gentle breeze.

Her power was intense, the clangs of both swords

against the Nnesutee's thin blade. In every clash, he thought the Nnesutee's sword would fail him, but it continually held. Appearing to move a fraction slower than the Ulaan, somehow his parries met her thrusts and swings.

Stealing a glance up into the tower, Philomene saw the Raja watching the duel with intensity, his eyes in constant motion. The Suten's eyes were obscured under his cowl, but it seemed to him that the man was grinning.

He turned back to the duel just in time to see the Nnesutee rolling beneath the Ulaan's double sword thrust, her eyes widening as blood sprayed into the air with a hiss. Had he waited another second, he would have missed it. Both swords clanged against the stone as her grip went slack, her head rolling to a stop near the circle's edge.

The Nnesutee flicked the blood off of his sword with a twist of his wrist, then briefly lowered his head in respect toward his fallen opponent. Two lines were visible on his back, dark spreading from them across the fabric of his robe, making it cling to his skin. He bowed towards the tower, giving a sword salute, then turned to face the Sibulla.

She stepped upon the circle to complete silence, the weight of her authority pulling every stunned eye towards her.

"Dris has spoken, and it is in the Raja of Ceidon's

favor. This arbitration is now concluded and recorded in the annals of kingdoms." Without a further word, she stepped down and walked toward the tower, the Master of Swords following behind.

It had happened so quickly that the Nnesutee was three paces off of Swordsman's Fate before the crowd began to cheer. The sound grew until words were indistinguishable in the roar.

Philomene drew a deep breath in disbelief. Could it be over? Had they actually won? He noticed the Nnesutee stopping, lifting his hand to someone in the crowd, and then noticed that the Raja was standing with a hand lifted in the same direction, a warm expression on his face. He spun searching through the gathered throng, and then grinned himself. There in the distance, with arm uplifted, was Jakgrim. Beyond the mixture of relief and exultation on the former Master of Sword's face, he looked quite well. He lowered his arm, bowed his head to the Raja, to Iskander, then turned, melting into the crowd.

He didn't see me, but it does my heart well to have seen him. I should have known he would come. His grin widened as he glanced back to the tower, then his brows raised in alarm. The Raja still looked in the direction that Jakgrim had gone, but the Suten Lord was no longer there.

11

CLOUDED SIGHT

Khiron practiced his sword forms on the deck, the glint of sweat covering his exposed torso. The Nnesutee sat nearby, quietly resting with his head tilted on one shoulder, his staff lying across his crossed legs.

"You have good form and balance, Khiron," the Nnesutee said. "Your forms are solid, and your footing sure."

Not sure how to respond to a blind man giving him a critique, he just frowned. "How do you do that? I mean, can you actually see?"

"Sound, smell, presence, air displacement; no matter how I would try to explain it, you wouldn't understand. Just take it as a fact; I am aware of what you are doing."

"Magery then."

The Nnesutee shook his head. "Does a fish need magery to extract oxygen from water or a trout need magery to climb out of the water and bury itself in mud to survive times of drought? No, it's an ability born of necessity and discipline, not the slightest bit of magery involved."

"Then it's something that can be learned?"

A chuckle. "I am all the evidence..."

Running footsteps caught the attention of both men, and they turned towards the cabin stairs.

Khiron's eyes widened as the Arat ran passed him and stopped before the Nnesutee in excitement.

"Did you see it? Did you see it?"

The Nnesutee grinned. "The probability that he would win was low, but our tribe has a way of superseding the odds."

"What happened?" Khiron asked.

The Arat turned to him, a wide smile on her face. "The Master of Swords of Zaim, he defeated the Ulaan in single combat!"

"What? The threat is over? You didn't know that was going to happen?"

She shook her head, distractedly. "It's difficult to see outcomes when it comes to Nnesutee and..."

Khiron motioned her silent as a sailor walked by, heading to the galley. No one spoke until the door closed behind him.

"There's nothing to worry about saying that name

now, Khiron," she said. "They let us live while on their island, so it's unlikely they would attack us."

"I wouldn't care if they were our blood-kin," he retorted. "Even if they gave us a pass, it doesn't mean they would extend it to the people who overheard us."

Her pout took him by surprise, disarming him, and for a moment, he forgot she was the Arat, and just thought of her as his daughter—the daughter he chose, and who had chosen him. A pang of remorse shot through him at the unjustness of it. She was under threat from so many, and it was unfair that someone so young should have to deal with such pressures.

He was about to apologize when her face went ashen. Just as suddenly, the Nnesutee sat up, straightening.

"What does this mean?" she asked the blind swordsman in a rush. "Do you understand this?"

"It is a convergence of power, young one. It is like a sand storm, and I do not see who emerges from its cloud."

"Who?" Khiron asked. "Emerges? From what? Are we about to be under attack? What in Dris' name are you talking about?" His questions ran into each other as if they were one sentence, irritation writ in every aspect of his expression.

Surprisingly, it was the Nnesutee who answered.

"Our friend from the Island is about to face one of

the Nine of the Ulaan. Soon they will be standing across from each other in mortal combat, and there is no sign as to who will walk away with their life." He turned his head fractionally towards the Arat. "Have you seen anything more than what I've shared?"

She nodded. "I see them standing across from each other like you do, but behind the Ulaan looks to be the hand of an Ancient." She shuddered. "Zaim is safe for now, but I fear for the fate of Gaia herself."

"There is much confusion ahead," the Nnesutee stood as he spoke, using his cane to pull himself up. "The battle that comes is irreversible, and I am blind to the events that follow."

Khiron felt helpless, his mind a blur of thoughts. "How long before this battle happens? Should we turn around and see if we can help?" He realized how foolish he sounded even before he finished the question.

Instead of being angry, the Arat rushed him, hugging him tightly, and he felt the trickle of her tears running down his skin. He hugged her back, trying his best to give her the comfort that he didn't feel.

"As of this moment," the Nnesutee said, "I see nothing past this battle which is to come. It is a convergence, and the future of Gaia rests on its outcome. For the first time since I was a child, I feel truly blind." His locks blew in the wind as he stared, open-eyed, into the distance.

"I see dragons," the Arat said through sniffles.

"That war," the Nnesutee said as he turned towards the galley, "like Gaia's future, rests on the outcome of this battle to come…or, so I believe."

Khiron didn't understand any of what was being said. It was beyond him, but he gripped the Arat's shoulders and pushed her from him so she could see him. "Look at me," he said. Her wet eyes looked into his. "No matter what happens, no matter what may come, I will be by your side."

She sniffled, trying to stop the tears from falling, and attempted to smile. "I know. I know. It's what keeps me going." She hugged him again, then pulled back, gathering herself.

"Where are you heading?" Khiron asked the Nnesutee, who was walking towards the galley.

"Let me share a lesson I learned long ago. When there is nothing you can do, never give in to despair. Find some food and eat, rest, and prepare for when there is something for you to do. This battle isn't ours, but our battles are coming soon enough. In the meantime, we should eat."

With that, the swordsman pushed open the galley door and disappeared inside.

Khiron looked at the Arat, and she looked at him, then both bolted after him.

12

A CULLING

The festivities were in full swing upon the lowlands. News of the Master of Swords' victory had reached the border of Zaim, and celebration broke out across the landscape like wildfire.

Swordsman's Fate was empty, the blood washed off the gray slate, and the body taken into the Ulaan's care. The Mount of Ceidon had been cleared of everyone who did not live there other than the Ulaan. The royal guard was posted to keep out the curious eyes of those who did.

Zatrin Bei sat in the short tower, relieved but concerned. She was upon the throne to the Raja's left, the Master of Swords on the right, with Philomene standing behind him.

A figure rushed through the soldiers towards the

tower. It was Rephna. Before she could arrive, the message she carried was already evident.

Nine Ulaan, all in leather armor and in cowls with no cloaks, approached Swordsman's Fate. Somehow, in the time that elapsed between the issuance of the Suten's challenge and now, Ueeha had gathered the rest of the Nine. They seemed to glide across the distance with speed.

The Ulaan swordsmen, who had all been sitting in meditation, abased themselves in unison as the Nine passed. Ueeha stepped upon Swordsman's Fate while the other eight stood side-by-side just outside the circle's perimeter.

Ueeha's confidence was evident as she spoke. "Where is the Suten pretender who thought he could challenge the Nine?" The response was immediate.

"Nine of the Ulaan, you are deemed unworthy." The Suten Lord's voice tolled out from behind her.

Startled, she spun to see him standing center circle, the Suten called Neftii standing beside him.

He looked at her with a predatory glare, threat pulsing in his singular regard. His voice was a winter breeze. "As Suten, we honor the protocols of swords, but we have a matter elsewhere that needs to be addressed," he said. "Accordingly, I offer this boon. My duel with Ueeha will be in the tradition of Dris. After that," he glanced at the rest of the Nine, "you may suspend the rules of tradition by declaration if you deem it is necessary."

"What?" Ueeha's expression was utter disbelief.

"I challenged the Ulaan," he said, letting his cloak fall to the stone, "not Ueeha of the Ulaan. As you lead as Nine, you were challenged as Nine. That you all have come makes this straightforward and efficient. I give you my thanks."

In the short tower, Zatrin Bei gasped. *Mother of Night! He knew she would bring them! Dris forfend!* Her shock was interrupted by one of the gathered Nine, who laughed awkwardly. His voice was like water coursing through gravel.

"We are not your lessors, Suten, despite your airs and graces."

Another voice spoke from the Nine, this one female. "I recognize that you bear a Katal master sword, so I know you are a master of note. He does not make many. That said, we do not wish an all out war with your kingdom. I object to this challenge unless we are absolved of guilt and assured of no reprisals from your Isle. To send a swordsman such as you to Nihil's realm is a tremendous pity, but that decision was made before we arrived."

"A voice of reason amongst you," he said. "You, I may spare." He turned to the short tower where the Sibulla and others sat, their joy of the earlier victory washed away by a mixture of fear and awe. "Sibulla, as you are my witness, I absolve the Ulaan from the outcome of this duel and declare that there will be no retaliation from the Suten in response to such." He looked at the Ulaan woman who had spoken, "Is that sufficient?"

She nodded in affirmation.

Zatrin felt like screaming. It was clear to her now that the Suten had planned this from the beginning. Once again, he had used her role as a Sibulla to give his actions validity. Her hands clenched in frustration. Whether what was transpiring was right or wrong, the Sibulla were the arbiters of kingdoms, not their pawns. This must never happen again.

At a look from her Lord, Neftii backed from the circle, leaving the two combatants alone.

A breeze blew, the scent of jasmine in the air. His eyes squarely upon Ueeha, the Suten Lord spoke. "Ulaan, prepare yourself for Nihil's embrace."

The bell rang from the short tower, and Ueeha lunged with an impossibly fast double-sword thrust. The Suten deflected both swords with a side-step and swipe from his scabbarded sword, striking the woman in the side of her neck with extended fingers as he shifted past her. She fell to the stone with a disturbing crunch, lifeless.

Every one of the Ulaan stood, hands on their sword hilts.

Zatrin stood distractedly, trying to replay what she

had just witnessed in her head. *Impossible! This is impossible. He never even drew his sword. She is one of the Nine!*

The Suten Lord stood calmly as two of the Ulaan swordsman checked on their fellow leader. They looked up in complete astonishment and confirmed the obvious.

His voice cut through the air like a sharpened blade. "Shall we suspend the rules?"

Silence.

Zatrin stared transfixed. The Suten's face and form were a vision of perfection: like an artist's masterpiece, like a god amongst the throngs. She had suppressed it before, but now, at this moment, his allure was almost palpable.

Movement. Another of the Nine ascended Swordsman's Fate. The man was as tall as the Suten and moved like a panther. He assumed a low stance, holding both swords above his head: one directly held vertically, its blade pointing towards the sky, and the other on a downward angle. Seeming to move with the bell, he attacked, his form perfect, swords simultaneously striking high and low.

What seemed a simple circular side-step took the Suten beyond the slashes, his elbow slamming into the side of the man's head as his strike filled the space the swords had just vacated. The crack of the blow split the silence of the night. The Ulaan spun, tried desperately to find his feet, and then collapsed. His body convulsed briefly before it lay motionless.

Zatrin's jaw dropped. The gathered Ulaan were mumbling now, the sound of swords freeing from their scabbards filling the air throughout the Mount.

The Suten Lord motioned to Neftii, and she moved before the tower entrance, taking a defensive position by the door, a naked dagger in each hand.

Zatrin fought back a growing fear. *Dris forfend! He stands as if their skill is inconsequential; stands elevated above the rulers of their people as if he's their better. He waits, yet no one ascends the circle to challenge him! Me'ett's merciful gaze be upon us; he has stolen something from them. Their beliefs are falling like the two who grow cold upon the circle. He did this for it to be witnessed. Now that it has, he waits for them to say it, and they will. Opassin have mercy, they will! Nihil's borders are growing fat this day, and somewhere that bastard is smiling.*

The Suten spoke. "You would all draw your swords against me?" His expression was one of a master to a stunted pupil as he looked amongst them. "What is the rule of Dris in warfare when a person draws a sword?"

That was the final push. She sighed as she prepared herself to witness what must follow.

A cry full of malice came from one of the Nine, "I suspend the rules! Ulaan atta—"

Before he could finish the sentence, the Suten Lord was in their midst.

Zatrin was both horrified and held captive by the scene in front of her. It was a thing of terrible beauty.

The Suten was everywhere, his dance a blur of exquisite technique. Leverage, timing, and brutal efficiency marked his every move. It took a moment for her to register that the Suten's sword still lay on Swordsman's Fate, where it rested on his cloak. It was not needed. A whirlwind of kicks, punches, breaks, locks, and throws was eradicating what was considered the most feared swordsmen throughout all of Gaia.

Where the Nnesutee looked to be a step slower than the Ulaan he faced, the Suten looked a full step quicker than his attackers.

Blades jabbed into empty air or found themselves sheathed in the bodies of their fellows. It was as if it was choreographed. Swordsmen whose balance rivaled the greatest of dancers stumbled and tripped into each other, and as many Ulaan were felled by their own as by the Suten Lord himself.

He was a lion amongst sheep: coiled muscle exploding into cartilage, flesh, and bone. He tore into them without pause, a dance of death with no movement wasted.

Her mind raced numbly, trying to comprehend what it beheld, her mouth agape.

Here was an artist, the sound of contact and expelled breath a symphony of release from this world. Here was a killer, a weapon, terrible to behold, yet too beautiful in craft and form to be denied. In less than the span of fifty breaths, he stood alone. Of all the Ulaan bodies, only the one who had spoken caution yet breathed.

A tear fell from Zatrin's eye. She was struck dumb.

Darkness fell, a night chill settled in.

Zatrin, the Raja, Philomene, and the Master of Swords emptied out of the short tower to find the Suten Lord donning his cloak, his sheathed sword now secured on his side. His presence dominated, drawing their attention to him and away from the macabre sea of corpses that surrounded them. Instead of looking exultant as Zatrin expected, sorrow marked his visage.

"What you have witnessed tonight was necessary," he said. "Remember this." His regard shifted to the Raja. "Remember that which you spoke earlier today. We are servants of our people and servants of all people when the need arises. Gaia and the Walled Dimensions have benefited today, though they know it not."

A breeze washed over them, the smell of the sea tangy and crisp. In the silence, sounds of music and celebration were discernible, a reminder of the world beyond the Mount.

The Suten Lord looked reflective, his voice carrying fatigue. "Take care, Iskander. Master of Swords is a title that is appropriate for you. Wear it well. When it is time, you will be welcomed in Suten. Old wounds have healed, and the shores of Suten now embrace you."

The Nnesutee's stance suddenly stiffened. He bowed his head, his head lifting to reveal wet cheeks.

Philomene the Guileless was struggling to pull the surviving Ulaan clear from the bodies, his eyes twitching as if his mind was failing to cope with what he had seen. His struggle eased, and he looked up to see Neftii helping to lift the Ulaan's limp body. He nodded his thanks, averting his eyes from her beautiful face.

They moved the Ulaan to an open area near the tower, and then Neftii joined her Lord on Swordsman's Fate.

Zatrin walked to the edge of the ring, her legs feeling heavy. "All was witnessed and is in order, Suten Lord. I say again, all is in order."

"I am pleased to hear it," he said.

"I believe," she said, " I understand what happened here, why you did what you did. I will record it accordingly."

His smile was unexpected. "I would presume no less from a Sibulla." He turned from her. "Neftii…"

Stepping in front of her lord, the woman's almond-shaped eyes went dull, and the atmosphere charged. The hair on the back of their necks stood taut as waves of magery blurred the air like heat in a desert plain. It rolled from her outstretched hands, striking the bodies of the dead Ulaan with force. There was a keening sound as the magery grew thick and darkened until the night air looked bright in comparison. With a staggering suddenness, the sound ceased. The magery dissolved into nothingness, revealing mounds of dust blowing away in the wind.

"Dris' Beard!" Philomene exclaimed. "I thought you said that the Ulaan were immune to magery. They tore through my fellow mage core without as much as a burn."

"Resistant," the Suten Lord said, "not immune. Dris made it so that they negate magery. But as in most things, it's all a matter of how much."

Neftii's eyes had returned to normal, and she locked them on the Nnesutee's own. She gave him the slightest of nods, and turned, her movement almost gentle.

Tears fell liberally from the Nnesutee's eyes. He bowed to them both, his hands clasped tight, resting on the small of his back.

A vertical rent split the air in front of the Suten, opening to reveal an obsidian landscape beyond. The Suten Lord spoke as if answering a question. "One does not need ships when they can walk the dimensions. We are the Suten." He turned away from them, and he and Neftii walked through. The rent closed, leaving all in stunned silence, standing alone in the whistling breeze.

13

PSIONIA'MATRI

Zatrin Bei sat on a plush divan in the Priory at the seaside city of Chalice, her thoughts far from the echoes of the crashing waves and crying gulls; lost from the scent of salty air and seaweed. Within the consecrated stones of her sacred Order's outpost, her abilities were at their peak, her focus supreme.

The large stones of this inner chamber radiated warmth. Ornate images were carved directly into the stone face, the line of the craftsmanship glowing a soft blue revealing the active warding protecting the space.

The room was cylindrical in shape. A divan with plush pillows sitting in its center was its only furnishings. An oval window high above facing east was its sole source of natural light. The window had no frame but looked to have been carved directly out of the stone blocks themselves, too high to reach without a tall ladder.

A casting stone in each hand, the black spheres reflecting blue in her open palms, Zatrin began to elevate from the divan. She rose slowly, smoothly, coming to rest with her body suspended mid-air directly across from the oval window. An adumbration of pale blue marked her outline, her eyes closed and palms outstretched. The edges of the window radiated the same color, the outside of the window turning opaque, the room suddenly in a different place.

"You did well, Soaring Sparrow. You have witnessed much." The voice came from everywhere, the voice of the Psionia'Matri.

"It is as you said, Mother of Sight. The Arat must be brought to Atori before your presence. Her abilities are," she paused, "formidable."

"What conclusions have you drawn from what you have witnessed, Soaring Sparrow?"

Zatrin felt discomfort for the first time since she left Mount Ceidon, for the ramifications of what she saw could be problematic for her Order.

"Mother of Sight, I believe the Kingdom of Suten has masterfully countered the will of the Ancient Dris by disabling the Ulaan kingdom's leadership directly. If what the Suten Lord said was true, the Ancient had planned to claim the Gaia dimension for himself through the Ulaan, and this had been a long time in the planning. The Nine didn't teach one of Dris' catechisms to the Ulaan masses, breaking the laws of the great Ancient. It is such an unconscionable act, it could only have been sanctioned by the Ancient himself. Using Dris' own scriptures against him, the Suten Lord was able to pronounce sentence and execute judgment without raising the ire of Dris or any of the other Ancients—"

"Correction, Soaring Sparrow," the Psionia'Matri interrupted, "the Suten Lord used Dris' own teachings to validate his judgment, and he also used us."

Zatrin swallowed hard, her stomach suddenly light. "Yes, Mother, he used me. He used our Order."

Silence lingered before the Psionia'Matri responded. "It is well, Soaring Sparrow. Each of the Ancient's candles still burns blue in the inner temple. None have snuffed out nor changed their color. Balance is maintained, and the Qio'Nadri is still recognized by all major entities in the Walled-Dimensions, and beyond. What I witnessed through you demonstrated that you had no other recourse, and your honor remains unstained, as does ours."

A sudden release of breath. She hadn't realized she had been holding it. Her voice faltered as she spoke. "Thank you, Mother of Sight. Thank you."

"It is well, Soaring Sparrow," the voice was stern yet warm. "Of all of your sisters, you have always had keen insight. What else have you concluded? Leave nothing out."

Zatrin was angry with herself. None of this would be necessary if she had given her leader unfettered access to her thoughts as the events transpired. She understood this report was a rebuke that she had placed upon herself.

"There is a major shift happening in the cosmos involving all the Walled Dimensions. The Suten are once again active in Gaia, but the brilliance revealed in the Suten Lord's actions leads me to believe it is for the purpose of protecting Gaia in the midst of this shift. I don't believe the Suten represent a threat to our Order, but rather, I believe the contrary."

She opened her eyes, and the image of an older woman, legs crossed in like manner, hovered across from her. Her skin was unlined, but her eyes held the weight of Ages. Brown hair with grey streaks was tied into a braid, a purple gem hung heavily from a silver necklace over a silk shift. The Psionia'Matri looked at her without expression, but her focus on her words and their import was apparent.

Zatrin continued. "The Suten sought to make a statement, and they used Mount Ceidon as the platform to achieve that end. During the battle, I sensed the presence of more than one Ancient. When the Suten left, the weight of their presence left with him. I was disoriented by the suddenness of it."

"All were present, Soaring Sparrow. I saw the spiraling hawk, the butterfly that teetered on the tower roof's edge. The leaf that fell unnaturally slow from the treetop and landed on a lower branch perfectly balanced, and the yellow flower that bloomed just before the Nnesutee's battle. And then there was the lone wolf that lay atop the palace itself."

Zatrin gasped. "Nihil was present—" Her words fell into awed silence.

"They all were," she said again. "That many Ancients in one place leaves no doubt that all Ancients were present or represented in some manner. All powers of consequence were witnesses, just as I was compelled to witness through you."

"Me'etts' mercy."

"What is further, a war has erupted amongst dragon-kind. In the face of the furor and ramifications that may result from that fray, that they all paused to watch a solitary duel..."

Zatrin's mind raced. The chaotic energy that had rippled through the cosmic. The release of power at the Suten Lord's pronouncement in the throne room. The feeling of inadequacy that colored her every move upon arriving at Mount Ceidon. The Suten's impatience before he departed. It all made sense now. She had witnessed the declaration of a kingdom to war. The Suten Lord was addressing powers well beyond the paltry kingdoms of Gaia, and the powers had listened and responded with pause. *Just who are these Suten? They are Gaian, just as we are, but they have become a force beyond us. And I thought I understood what I witnessed...'*

When she spoke again, it was with clarity. "Mother of Sight, I see now that every action the Suten Lord took touched multiple dimensions. In siding with Zaim against the Ulaan he protected them, and in honoring the Qio'Nadri, he honored us, reinforcing the protections which we already operate under."

The Psionia'Matri smiled. "It seems that fortune continues to grant honor upon our Order." Her expression saddened. "It will not always do so. We must learn more about the Suten. Since they closed their borders nearly a century ago, we have had no contact."

"I sought to explore, for I was able to track the Arat to their Isle. Sight was denied me, and I was rebuffed by the mere command of a Nnesutee."

"Fear not. Sight of their Isle is blocked from us all. No seer, mage, or sensitive has any sight of their whereabouts, something that didn't come to my notice until your attempt. I have dispatched one of your sisters to the Isle in person to seek an audience. That the Suten Lord honored the Qio'Nadri convinced me that the risk is warranted."

Zatrin Bei bowed her head in understanding.

"Concerning the Nnesutee, they are cousins to the Suten and have royal blood in their veins. Their numbers are small, probably less than two dozen to date and only one or two are known to have power great enough to "rebuff" our powers."

Alarm rushed through her features. "But the Nnesutee was with the Arat!"

"Rest, Soaring Sparrow. The Arat still lives. The Nnesutee live with honor, and it seems that this one has decided to accompany her on her journey, at least for now. His intentions are unknown, but the death of the Arat is not his purpose, for she yet lives. She is now your assignment. Find her and bring her to me, as you have said. With Opassin's touch, we may be able to protect her before the attention of those now focused on the War of Dragons falls upon her."

She bowed her head. "As you command Mother of Sight."

The Psionia'Matri was silent, her gaze penetrating. "What troubles you? I sense imbalance."

A delayed exhale. "Mother, I still struggle to believe what I witnessed. That any swordsman could be skilled enough to defeat one of the Nine, much less all of them and an Ulaan contingent—" her voice fell. "It should not be possible."

The Psionia'Matri's eyes became distant as if in memory, then sharpened. "Yes, it is rare to see anyone achieve mastery on such a level. His martial skill is exceptional. His strategy defeated them as soundly as his skill."

Strategy? "Mother, I don't underst—"

"The Arat is under threat. She is garnering attention too soon," the Psionia'Matri said. "Find and secure her quickly. I am sending sisters to assist you. I cannot emphasize it enough, move with haste."

She bowed her head. "As you command Mother of Sight." When she looked up, the image of the Psionia'-Matri was gone.

Descending to the divan, the blue adumbration that marked the room faded, the window revealing a darkening sky.

She became aware of a chill in the air, heard the dance of waves at eventide, felt the salty humidity in air. The cushions were cool to the touch, her leather armor laid out on the dressing bench in the antechamber, the wool shift leaving the flesh of her calves exposed. She stood on the bare floor and walked toward the door, her casting stones held in one hand.

Questing, she nodded to herself. The Crest, the Raja's private ship, was still anchored off the shore. She had not paused to eat or rest once she arrived, but had traveled with haste to the priory to communicate with the Psionia'Matri without interference. It seemed that she would need the Raja's vessel for a little longer. *Rest is not to be mine tonight. Arat, I am coming for you. Me'ett keep you safe until I find you.*

14

FAITH

The temperature dropped steadily as the night took root. A soft spray filtered through the air, the cool moisture leaving a sheen across the deck. The Nnesutee sat wrapped in his cloaks, head lowered, breathing deeply. His walking staff laid across his thighs, supporting his forearms as he rested.

He and the Arat had sensed the Suten's victory, and the cloud which darkened their sight was lifting.

The Arat had gone to her cabin shortly after the suns had set, and Khiron had retired to their cabin not long thereafter. The boat had long stilled, the crew in their quarters. Only he, the Captain, and a seaman were topside, surrounded by sound wafting from the passing sea.

He could hear the even breathing below, sensing whispers of secrets from Khiron and aspects of the Arat's power as she slept. He frowned. Her magery signature had changed from just days ago, a coursing stream which flowed stronger and had grown in depth. Her short time on the Isle of Suten had grounded her and she did not yet have the maturity to keep it hidden.

He was aware that Philomene the Guileless had kept the young seer's power cloaked since her birth. The Raja's advisor had thought his act was unknown, but seers of power felt the entrance of her presence into this world from her first breath. The subsequent silence led most to feel that the child had died, but he had followed her trail to Zaim's Dunn Quarter years ago. He had felt the toddler's nascent abilities despite it being covered in a complex magery current and knew the day would come when he would have to make a decision.

As she grew in age and in power, Philomene's desire to protect the young seer had exceeded his ability to do so. Her wise prognostications on storms and other things had made her popular with the citizenry, but knowledge of her abilities remained local. Farmers were not quick to share things that benefitted them with outsiders. When the Nnesutee felt the lapse in her protection, he knew that the long-awaited time had come. Seer Mages like himself were rare, and represented a threat to all depending on their decisions. He would either have to kill her or to protect her and it led him to do the same.

With the Arat's current inability to obscure her growing power, she would soon attract unwanted attention, to him as much as to her if he continued to travel with her. She would have to grow in maturity to be able to keep her abilities hidden from those sensitive enough to notice them, or her life would be a short one. If she was going to survive, she would have to become more like him, and that would require training. It would require time; time they didn't have.

The ship creaked and groaned as it rode the waves. He sat lost in thought, shadowed beneath the lightened visage of the broken moon. Fish occasionally broke the surface of the water, the soft splashes marking their journey. The salty sea smelled sweet, a tangy taste in the air. The moon stood prominently in the night sky, mere moments from reaching its zenith.

The Suten Royal had grown in ability since he was last in his presence. He had felt the disciplined control of immense power, the undeniable ambiance of his presence, and wondered if the man's skill had surpassed that of his elder brother who was the best swordsman on the Isle in his memory.

Then there was Neftii. The well of her power had grown deep, and her beauty transcended sight. He sensed her regard on the beach, and in it he had felt an emotion he had only hoped for. Now that he was sure of it, he was struck by his uncertainty of what to do next. Timelines were mostly unreadable for Suten and had been for as long as he could remember. Slight hints of possibility teased at him but eluded him just the same. Yet from deep within him, he felt that their paths would cross again. An unbidden grin formed on his lips.

He grew mentally silent, searching and finding the heartbeats of the Captain, the crew, his fellow travelers, the fish near the ocean's surface, and then his grin grew wide.

Five shadows silently climbed over the rail, clothes matted against their flesh. They scanned the deck, locating the captain on the high bridge piloting the ship with his back to them. Unsheathing long daggers, they stealthily approached him when a shadow rose before them. They froze.

Blurs of movement in the dark. Swift sounds of slicing through air. Dull thuds of falling limbs. Light splashes of weights dropped into dark waves. Then stillness.

The Nnesutee stood by the railing, cleaning his sword on the clothes of the headless body which lay before him, then tossed the corpse overboard to join the rest. He sheathed his hidden sword.

No movements or stirring, no sounds that were out

of place. He grinned. Everything was as it should be. He had made his decision.

Unscrewing the bottom of his staff, he pulled out a small tube. Unstoppering it, he emptied the entire contents out in a wide arc. Not affected by the breeze, it descended onto the deck, dissolving all the liquid it touched. When the suns crested the morning rise, he was in his cabin sleeping silently as if he hadn't slept in months.

A BEAD of perspiration detached from the group gathered on Philomene's forehead. It slowly journeyed down his hilly brow to hang suspended from his chin. The mage was motionless, the palms of his hands on his knees as he sat erect on crossed legs.

Another bead broke from the rank, following in step. It rolled down the now marked trail to join with the first, their mutual weight breaking their grip as they fell, disappearing into the darkening fabric of his silken trouser-leg. The air was thick, stuffy, the windowless room heavy with the spicy scent of the lone candle which illuminated the unfurnished chamber. A continual hum resonated through the stone.

He could feel the dynamics of the Arat's power, despite the widening distance. Her unique signature had far outgrown his Order's ability to mask it.

Keeping their work from her knowledge had been a challenging feat. With their numbers winnowed down to a paltry four, all he could do for her now was to pray to Opassin, the Ancient of Fortune, for his favor.

These observations danced, barely perceptible, upon the edges of his consciousness. His mind was filled with thoughts of another.

The Suten Lord's battle with the Ulaan at Swordsman's Fate had been incomprehensible, and the subsequent magery used by the man's Second was terrifying. What he had witnessed should not have been possible, and yet, it had been accomplished with apparent ease.

He replayed the scenes over and over in his mind, seeking explanation or even a hint of something he may have missed. He found nothing: no tricks, no deceit. There had only been unimaginable martial artistry from one, and unmitigated power from the other. It was logically unacceptable.

The dissolution of the Ulaan had stolen his confidence. The removal of the evidence of their existence had left him shaken to his core.

He had been stunned, had even balked at the pericope of Catechism Eleven which he remembered when the Suten Lord accused the Ulaan leader of hiding it from their people. *"Stand not before a Suten sword, for its blade will not be dulled."* His understanding of that text now differed vastly from what it had prior.

A sense of light, a cool draft, and the scent of fresh

air ripped him from his thoughts. He opened his eyes to see torchlight flooding the room as the door continued to open, a silhouette taking form within the frame.

"Master, the Great Raja seeks your presence."

He mustered a sluggish nod as he willed strength back into his body. He hadn't slept since the battle, and the lack of rest was apparent.

The silhouette disappeared replaced by two who were obviously carrying something, their arms full. As his sight adjusted, he felt the heat from the towel being pressed upon his face, smelled the lather spread where the towel had been and heard more than felt the blade sliding across his cheeks.

His thoughts concretized into the present, and as the servants finished their work, he felt more like himself. They lifted a cup to his lips. When he swallowed the last of the acrid tea, his strength had returned. Swiftly donning the fresh robe presented, he made his way to the throne room.

The doors opened to reveal the Great Raja sitting alone in his blue finery, a look of complete relaxation writ plain in every feature. The man actually looked younger. As the doors closed, the Raja spoke.

"What a somber face you have, my friend. It's been days now. What has kept you from my presence?"

The one question I fear to answer and my liege asks it

without preamble. "Great Raja, I advise," he drew the word out like a strand of cotton, "caution."

The Raja sat back in his throne, the smile lifting from his eyes. "Continue."

Walking across the throne room, Philomene bowed to the Raja and then stood before him. "The Suten, they are a great ally, but they represent many unknowns." He let the thought linger.

"I understand your concern," the Raja said, nodding his head in agreement. "The Suten's sudden arrival at such an opportune moment could seem suspect to anyone, but I trust the Suten Lord's words, regardless of what his motive to come was." He paused, seeing his advisor's staid expression. "You remain unconvinced."

Philomene swallowed hard, clearing his throat before replying. "I am awash in concerns, Mighty Raja. The Suten woman who was slain by the Ulaan, why was she categorizing our soil types? How did she defend herself against two Ulaan single-handedly if she was just an academic or researcher? For Dris' sake! Our best barely slowed the Ulaan advance... It was almost as if the Suten were toying with them, and us. Then, the Suten Lord spoke of your esteemed father, claiming that they had been close friends, thereby—"

"Maneuvering me," the Raja finished the logical implication Philomene's rationalization. "Worry not, I take no offense at your words. I have considered these things, but have arrived at different conclusions than you. Come, my friend." He rose from the throne and walked to the Steep Bay. "What do you hear?"

Philomene followed, fighting his initial irritation at the question, stilling his thoughts to listen. His eyes tightened in concentration, and then slowly relaxed. "Other than birdsong and the far sound of construction, nothing my lord."

The Raja grinned. "I hear peace, and what I hear externally, I also feel within. Peace, Philomene." He breathed in deeply and exhaled as if savoring the air. "Maybe it is an attribute of royal sensitivity, but I heard no malice or duplicity within the Suten Lord's words. What he said, he meant, and I know this as surely as I know myself."

Philomene's thoughts screamed to be heard: the Arat's departure, the coming of the Ulaan and the Suten, the inhuman skill, the Ancient-like power, the precarious inadequacy of their kingdom in a faith that extols power...

Dris forfend, that was it.

The Raja had accused him of feeling inadequate concerning the Arat's power, believing he thought his position was at risk. The Raja had been incorrect, but there had been no need to correct him. Now, the stark reality was that in the face of what he had seen from the Ulaan and then the Suten, he felt more than inadequate; he felt fear. For himself, his Raja, and all of Zaim, he was afraid. Eyes fixing on a flock of birds that changed formation and direction as one, he said nothing.

"My friend," the Raja said with an uncharacteristic gentleness, "we have protection from two kingdoms - Chalice, and now the Isle of Suten - and these protections have bought us time. Time for you to rebuild your mage corps. Time for our Master of Swords to train a proper militia. Time for us to better the lives of all in Zaim. Time for us to gather intelligence and to focus on that which we can accomplish."

Philomene flinched. The Raja had rested his hand on his shoulder, something he had never done before. He turned to look at his Lord, surprised to see no signs of the weight that had threatened to topple him within his Raja's eyes. He saw a quiet confidence there, an assurance that he had not seen since the Raja's youth.

"It is well with us, my friend," the Raja said. "What the Suten Lord did was greater than you realize. I have known the burden of command for most of my life, and over the years, I've learned to be aware of the subtle shifts in that burden." His gaze lifted. "There is honor in the Suten Lord, an honor that my father sought to teach me. The Suten has a depth of character that grounds reality and gives assurances that overcome doubt. It is this depth that gives me confidence in our safety as a kingdom, for I believe what he did was a gift."

"My lord, I…"

"Ponder on this," the Raja said. "The Suten could have waited until after the Ulaan had defeated us before he came, or he could have placed Zaim under the Suten standard after defeating the Ulaan at Swordsman's Fate, yet he did neither. No, I trust the Suten Lord, and see his coming as a boon."

The soft ring of a bell ran through the throne room.

"I have summoned Iskander and would like your counsel afterward."

He nodded.

They turned to watch the silent entrance of the Master of Swords. Iskander seemed to glide with an inner dignity, coming to a halt at the center of the room. He bowed, waiting silently.

"Master of Swords," the Raja said, "your interaction with the Suten seemed incredibly personal."

"It was an honor to be in their presence, Great Raja. I've had no prior contact, but some of my tribe have. Our families share a history."

"Familial?"

"After a fashion, Great Raja."

The Raja waited for something more, but when the Master of Swords remained silent, he decided to change tact.

"Philomene and I are awed by your defeat of the

Ulaan swordsman. It has been held for decades that they could not be defeated in direct combat. That you are a master swordsman is beyond question, and that you serve Zaim is something I bless Driss for continually."

The Master of Swords gave a short bow. "Thank you, Great Raja. To serve such an honorable ruler and kingdom is a blessing in itself."

"As a master swordsman, I am sure you perceived things differently than a ruler with average skill with a blade would, or even a mage like Philomene, for that matter."

The Master of Swords nodded his agreement.

"It is for your insight that I've requested your presence, as I feel inadequate to the task of discerning what happened at Swordsman's Fate."

"Any summons by the Great Raja is an honor," he said with genuine respect in his tone. "I have awaited your summons on the matter since your healers saw to my wounds."

The Raja smiled.

Philomene once again felt fortunate that this man had accepted the role of Master of Swords. Jakgrim would have to be honored again in some way for his recommendation.

"In the battle between the Suten Lord and the Ulaan," the Raja asked, "what did you see? Was the Suten's skill that much better than his opponents?"

"His skill was superior, Great Raja, but his strategy was much more so."

Philomene's eyes widened in anticipation, but the Raja remained calm, his expression steady.

"The Suten Lord was quicker than they, but he also increased his speed by slowing theirs. He assessed their strengths and took them away. He found their weaknesses and exploited them."

"Weaknesses?"

"May I speak freely, Great Raja?"

"You are our Master of Swords. I would have you speak in no other way."

The Master of Swords' expression lightened with a pride only one who understands skill can display. "The reputation of the Ulaan is widely known. When was the last time they experienced someone attacking them? Despite their skill, when have they ever trained for a single swordsman engaging them en masse? How long did disbelief cloud their minds when they saw him drop his sword to attack? How much did fear steal their confidence in how he defeated the Nine, the best of their number? Great Raja, what the Suten Lord did was beyond masterful; it was sublime."

"But what of the two individual duels he had?" Philomene interjected. "The speed and accuracy he displayed? How was that humanly possible?"

The Master of Swords regarded him. "He is the swiftest swordsman I have ever witnessed, yet he still slowed them. Aesthetics is both a weapon and a shield, as is anger, when in a master's hand. The Suten's mastery is beyond Dojon rankings. The skill he displayed, less than a handful of swordsman throughout history have been the equal, if any."

"Thank you," the Raja said to the Master of Swords. "You have given us much to consider. Once again, Zaim is in your debt."

"There is no debt, Great Raja. Honor requires service, and the swordsman's purpose has always been peace. I hope I was able to help bring peace to your minds. I am honored that I was able to meet the Suten Lord. Being in the presence of one of that level of skill was humbling. As Master of Swords, I have received the greater portion and am bettered by the honor." With another deep bow, he turned and left the throne room.

The song of the birds was carefree, wafting into the space vacated by the swordsman. Both the Raja and Philomene stood awash in the serenity of the moment.

The Raja looked content, a man whose burdens had been considerably lightened and who was at peace with himself and his purpose.

Philomene was contemplative yet tense. He didn't understand what the Master of Swords meant by aesthetics as a weapon, but the import of what the Raja had shared and the Master of Swords had revealed had given him grounding.

Incrementally, his frown lifted, and as he bathed in the chorus of nature's choir, his shoulders fell. He finally felt the sleep that had eluded him since Swordsman's Fate beckoning him.

"Great Raja, may I have your leave?"

A broadening grin. "Granted."

15

———

BLADE'S KISS

Darkness, then light.

Four candles came to life in unison, the sudden illumination revealing three circles drawn onto the dark basalt floor: one circle within another, within another. At their epicenter knelt a man.

Nothing marked him as extraordinary in any way. He wasn't old. He wasn't young. He was neither fit nor frail. His hair was of average length, face neither pleasant nor plain. Nothing marked him as a mage. Nothing announced him as an assassin.

The candles were widely spaced, placed to create a square perimeter that encapsulated the circles. No ceiling was visible; no walls to give the space context. All seemed infinite, the man a mere mote adrift on an endless sea.

A spicy aroma filled the air as smoke from the candles rose high and then began to join. Swirling and billowing, flashes illuminated from within as if clouds were at war, lightning bolts hidden within the fray.

The man leaned his head back to face the smoke, which had formed into the shape of a massive face looking down directly above him. It spoke, its voice the sound of rolling thunder.

"The Arat still lives."

An unremarkable voice responded with an even tone. "The Arat was hidden in the kingdom of Zaim and now is on a ship. The Atiere reported that tracking her would be like tracking a whisper. They found her, but somehow, she was able to slip away."

"It is rare that Atiere hunters fail in an assignment." The columns of smoke continued to rise, vibrating visibly when the face spoke. "Yet they failed to fulfill their contract while sharing a ship with her. How do you account for this?"

"I understand that she has a sworn sword named Khiron protecting her, who served as a guard for the House of Laor before coming to Zaim. He is talented but should have proven minimal resistance at best. He should not have been a match for either of the Atiere, but definitely not both of them. How she still lives is a mystery."

"Failure is unacceptable, as is underestimation. The Atiere tribe will be punished."

"As you command. I dispatched an assassin cadre to fulfill the contract if, for any reason, the Arat survived. They will have executed the contract by now, so there is no need for concern."

The face contracted as if sucked backward by some rushing wind, followed by the sound of a long exhale. "Your assassin cadre has failed. The Arat still lives."

The expression contorted, the smoke growing darker by the moment. A heavy silence held, then the face surged downward. The man jumped at the explosion, the retort deafening as if lightning had struck inside the chamber. Its reverberation lingered within the stone, as if in fear. The smoke dispersed and then reformed to reveal the outer circle the man had drawn was no longer there.

"Before darkness, there was light. Before many, there was one. Before action, there was being." The voice boomed from every direction.

Again, the face surged downward. The man involuntarily flinched at the closeness of the attack, a wave of intense power rushing through the air. The smoke dispersed and reformed. The second circle was no longer drawn on the basalt. The voice seemed to come from a great distance through the ringing in his ears.

"Before chaos, there was balance. Before expression, there was essence. Before doubt, there was knowing."

A bead of sweat formed on the assassin's forehead, a mask of determination on his face.

"I sense your fear, assassin. Your arrogance is fleeing from you as if from a plague. You strove to be my agent knowing my price for failure." The face slammed downward a third time, crashing against the barrier. The smoke swirled around the inner circle as if a swarm of vipers around an egg, but when it dispersed, the circle still held.

Sweat cascaded down the assassin's forehead, genuine relief on his face. The smoke which lifted from the candles was normal now, the presence no longer in the chamber.

He exhaled slowly, working the tension out of his arms, and rested in the silence. As his strength returned, he said to the nothingness: "The Arat will die, O Ancient of War. I will dispatch her mysel—"

He felt twin pricks — one in his neck, the other in his chest — and then fell back to see a stunningly beautiful woman, her caramel skin and short white hair dreamlike. Two glints of silver shone in her hands, each at an angle, and her almond-shaped eyes fixed on him with no expression. She stepped into a slit in the air and was gone.

He heard himself whisper, "Who?" then his vision went dark. In the distance, he thought he heard the howl of a wolf.

COMING SOON...

Book Two of the Arat Series

"The Lament of Joy"

Fall of 2020

For updates, previews, and early access to new releases, go
to: liquidblackpress.com/join